Balish Lane's

Adventures
&
The Inferno Lord

Balish Lane's
Adventures
&
The Inferno Lord

Taksheel Desor

ADROIT
Adroit Publishers
New Delhi

ISBN : 978-81-87393-58-0

First Published in 2017

Published by
ADROIT PUBLISHERS
4675/21, Ganpati Bhawan, Ansari Road,
Daryaganj, New Delhi-110 002
Phone : 011-23266030

Exclusively Distributed by:

Akhil Book Distributors
4675/21, Ganpati Bhawan,
Ansari Road, Daryaganj
New Delhi, INDIA
Tel: 011-23266030

Typesetting—Akriti Graphic Solution, Delhi-110081
E-mail: arun263923@gmail.com
Cover and illustrations by —SAKSHAM KOHLI, Graphicos Designs
E-mail: graficos.design03@gmail.com
Printed at: Rajyoriya Prints, Delhi.

Dedicated to

My Grandparents and Parents

Contents

- CHAPTER -

1

The Miraculous Birth of Balish

It was the night of 21st November. The dark sky started raining. That night, a huge storm came. Outside the Lane's house, an infant, blown away due to the storm, fell down. It was God's miracle that the infant was safe.

The next morning, Mr. Lane with his sleepy eyes and long black beard, was going for walk. But just as he opened the front door, he shouted- Aargh! He saw the infant. He used to hate children. He had a child too, but he told his college-mate - Mr. Fernandez, who was standing outside for morning walk, to adopt him. Mrs. Lane ran to look what had happened, after she listened to the shriek of her husband. She understood the matter and requested Mr. Lane to adopt the child and not repeat the mistake they made by giving away the child earlier. He agreed finally, but said, "I won't accept this child as my son, and you will take care of him. Even you will do all the things for his comfort, not me at all". Mrs. Lane just happily agreed.

Still, she tried her best to make her grumpy husband accept the child, but he wouldn't. It hurt her so much that she decided to leave her house and go somewhere very far. During the journey, she pondered over and kept the child's name- ***Balish Lane***.

Ten years later, Balish was admitted in the Supersonic International School, where he could learn supersonic powers and spells. In this school, wizards and normal people both could join. But the condition especially for wizards was that they cannot use their powers on normal people at any cost, or else they would be put behind the bars. The special thing about Balish was that he was a normal child but he had powers of a wizard. The storm, in which he was saved by God, is an example that he is a normal wiz-person. His world was his mother. She hated her husband due to his inhuman behavior and did not want Balish to know that due to him, she left the home to take care of him. She hated her husband so much that she told that his father had died due to heart attack.

On his first day of school, he met many wizards and got scared of them, but gradually he overcame his fear and understood that they won't do anything to him, because they would not want to go behind the bars.

He met all his teachers in two days. He made many friends, and his three best friends were Alfred, Christopher, and Jack. The trio were good in studies and they were friendly too, so they would often play with Balish in the school ground. There were two grounds, one for the wizards to play their favorite game, Quidditch and one for the normal children (for baseball, cricket, and basketball). But Balish was very lucky, for he could play in both grounds as he was a normal wiz-person.

One day, Balish thought to call his friends for homework. Their home was through the jungle. Balish and his mother thought it would be a great idea to walk through the jungle and have fun, see the nature. So both Balish and his mother went together to call them. Often, the jungle was not haunted, but some said that the jungle is a home of a veteran and scary wizard, who was also called the **'Inferno Lord'**, as he could just throw a stroke of heat from his magical wand, and the one in front would be 'POOF - vanished'!. And unfortunately, that day was probably the last day of Balish's mother. Just in the middle of the forest, a strong gush of wind blew and the sky became dark, only in that part of the jungle. The Inferno Lord had approached! His target was mainly children and he could throw only one stroke of heat in the jungle and for second stroke, he needed 12 hours gap. He

targeted Balish. His mother quickly responded and came in front of Balish, sacrificing her life for the sake of Balish. The stroke was so strong that even the mother's ash also vanished. Only a deep but permanent scratch appeared on Balish's hand, and he ran for life.

* * *

- CHAPTER -

2

Supersonics' Teachers

He reached home, locked all the doors, shut the windows, and started crying deeply for his mother. He thought about the incident. He was sad. He was angry. He wanted to take revenge. Then onwards, he kept only one word in mind- REVENGE from Inferno Lord!

Very soon all his friends came to know about the sudden death of Balish's mother. They came closer to Balish, and Christopher, one of Balish's best friends, said 'Why don't you come to our house and stay there forever?' As Balish didn't know much about his early childhood, he agreed to stay there.

Everything was going very well but suddenly one day, the scratch on Balish's body starting hurting him. It started bleeding again. A purple glow was coming out of that scratch. Balish couldn't understand anything.

He put many medicines and bandages but nothing could stop the bleeding. 23 hours passed. Balish started losing his powers. As if his half energy had gone away. But suddenly something miraculous happened. Some energy flew and the glow stopped. Balish then understood that it is nothing but some magical power which has saved him. It was a fine day. In the Supersonics', Mr. Jorge, the history teacher was teaching in the class. He was the strictest teacher. He always showed off that he knew everything about history. He was just resuming his boring lesson when Harold, a curious little boy came to Mr. Jorge and asked a question.

'Mr. Jorge, how did Napoleon die? He asked.

The teacher got angry, because of his attitude, he took one stick and replied, 'Oh Harold, don't you know that you were a great king at that time and you only killed him? You fool, now go and sit on your seat.

Still Harold asked, 'Sir, please tell us, because you told us that you know everything about history'

After listening this, all the children laughed, including Balish. Just then the bell rung and it was time for lunch. There Balish and many first year students were sitting on the desks and benches. The senior students had a different section for lunch.

A wizard boy named Fredrick came and sat with Balish. He asked, 'Hey boy, where are you from? I want to experiment something on you. Are you a wizard'?

Someone had asked Balish for the first time whether he was he a wizard or what? So Balish just silently whispered, 'Yes'.

He pulled him to the Quidditch ground of wizards and just without wasting time, he pulled out his wand

and said to Balish, 'You're doomed'! But not even a flicker of his futile experiment harmed Balish. Balish laughed and then pulled out his wand and said, 'you will be more intelligent than ever'. He laughed continuously and came back to the hall. Fredrick was confused. But due to the intelligence that Balish gave, he came to know everything. Balish had done it to make him understand that the wand was held wrongly and his wand had a small crack too.

Balish then continued his studies until the last period and while returning home, he told Christopher about the incident that happened and he laughed too. By gossiping and talking, they reached home (Christopher's home).

At home, Mrs. Laurence (Christopher's Mother) was preparing dinner. 'Mom, why is dinner being prepared so early', Christopher asked.

She said, 'Dear Balish and Christopher, me and your father are going for dinner to Mr. Polska's house. They have got a posting to Austria, and he has organized a dinner where only parents are invited and the men may have a meeting too. So you both have dinner at the correct time, and if we are late, sleep too. You have school tomorrow - no'?

'Mr. Polska? Isn't he Jack's father? We would also surely go mom, he is our best friend', Christopher and Balish spoke together. But their mom had already ignored them and she went to get ready for the dinner. Both the friends were very upset. They too wanted to go to their best friend's house, and they were desperate. They thought and decided to go secretly, by disguising their faces. This could happen with the help of Balish's magical wand, which could expand in size and become a flying broom. So both put their hands together and said, 'Hooray. We will go to our best friend's house at any cost. We CAN'T miss the farewell party of our departing friend. We can, and we WILL go'!

However they didn't want to lie with Mrs. Laurence, but if it comes to the thing of Jack's farewell party, they had to go for the sake of their friendship.

At the Polskas' house, Jack was very sad for he couldn't invite his own best friends, Alfred, Balish and Christopher. He was sitting at a corner of his room, and just then his mother came. She said, 'I know why you are sad, darling. But what can I do? You know your father's habit. He's so selfish, and we can't question his decision, so please be quiet. I will let you talk and chat with them in Austria. Don't be sad'.

Jack knew that his mother is not wrong. He was aware of his obstinate father's habit and he cried in his heart and went down to give help for the dinner, which was going to be so boring for him. He could have gone to his friends' house for the last time, but he was just sitting quietly in his house. He had a hope that by hook or by crook, his friends would come to the party.

It was 7 O'clock in the evening. The settings were ready. The dinner was ready to be organized. In Christopher's home, since 5 O'clock, they both were trying how to change their faces and dresses, and they had almost learnt how to do that, however their mother was approaching upstairs to tell that she and dad were going.

Christopher heard the footsteps of his mother. He quickly shut down the laptop and hid all the items that were coming in action for their plan to go to Jack's farewell party.

She came and said the expected sentence, 'My darlings, I hope that you would do all the things I told you. If you do so, I would raise your pocket money by 5%'.

They were hypnotized by the sentence. They said in excitement, 'Whoa! raising of pocket money, that too by 5%! That means if our normal pocket money is 8 Euros, then our pocket money will increase and become 8.4 Euros! Yes mom, we will surely obey your advice. Bye and have a good dinner'!

They were very happy. However, they had to execute their plan, as money is not more precious than your friend. Money can go and the same can be earned, but good friends don't. So they started getting ready when the front door closed. They wore a strange outfit, but they didn't know that they are doing a blunder by wearing only that outfit. It was of a person who was very helpful to Mrs. Lane. It was of none other than Mr. Yanky, an elf who helped her to carry on her journey when she ran away from her house, leaving Mr. Lane. However, there was no news of Mr. Lane and for Mr. Yanky, some people said that a vehicle had collapsed on him and he died, so the kids unintentionally just put on the outfit and sat on Balish's wand, which expanded like a broom and they set off for their journey.

They didn't know what a great chaos they were about to create at Polskas' house, and they just went. In the middle of the journey, they saw their mother in the car and they just passed along them.

* * *

GHOST!
GHOST!

- CHAPTER -

3

Mayhem at the Dinner

They had almost reached Jack's house, but accidentally they hit a tree and their wand broke and again became small that is why they fell with a 'DOOM' on the ground. They lost consciousness and because of that, they were very late.

When they regained consciousness, Christopher saw his watch and it was 8 pm already. The dinner had obviously started and the guests already had snacks, which almost made their stomach full. Christopher as *Mr. Lane* and Balish as *elf Yinky*, were not aware of the fact of these people. They reached the Polska's house and went inside, wearing their invisibility cloak to just go inside. There were many guests. Then they saw Mr. and Mrs. Laurence.

Christopher just froze with fear and whispered to

Balish, 'Hey friend, we will not be caught no'? Balish said calmly, 'Chill bro. We can't be caught. We are wearing our invisibility cloaks. Nothing will happen to us'.

They were waiting for the dinner to be served, so that they could join the men and act to have a meeting.

The dinner had not yet served, and what was worse than that, that Mrs. Laurence took out her phone and called the landline number of their home. Christopher and Balish saw her and got really scared. Christopher told him, 'Because of you, we will be caught. Is your friend more important than rushing back home and receive the call'?

Balish got angry. He didn't speak, but the expression was clear on his face. He went somewhere away from Christopher, and sat. He said to himself, 'What a fuss he is making for a small thing'. He took a glass of coke from the tray. As no one could see him, he drank it. On the other side, Christopher was very worried. He saw his mother who was again calling the landline number and angrily cutting the call. He thought, 'Will mom think that we are playing games with loud voice, or we are dancing with the loudspeaker which Mr. Ambrose gifted us, or what'? This was troubling Christopher a lot. But then Jack came and his appearance disappeared all the trouble and tension off from Christopher's face.

He was taking the dinner without eating snacks. He was missing his friends a lot, which was very much visible on his face. Finally Balish came too and then they both joined the line, taking off their invisibility cloaks. No one saw them coming suddenly and their mission was successful. But not almost.

Just as the line finished, Mrs. Laurence saw Balish, appearing to be Mr. Lane and Christopher, who was in the get up of Mr. Yinky. She yelled,' Ghosts! Ghosts'! All the people were attracted by this. They saw them too. Before the kids could understand anything, the guests took off their shoe and threw it on them. There was a great mayhem here. As they had heard that Yinky and Mr. Lane who was Balish's father had died, they were surprised and they attacked on them. The kids were badly injured and somehow they ran.

They came to know that their wand had broken. They were wonderstruck. They were standing like a statue outside the house of Polskas'. They had two big problems. One, they couldn't meet Jack properly and the second was that how to go home back? As their wand has broken, they had no other way than walking back home. They first of all removed the outfit because of which they got beaten. They were still surprised that why did they beat them. Were they unexpected guests? No, No. Mr. Polska had organized this dinner openly. Then why did they beat them? The secret was very big. They were adventurous kids and they had to somehow come to know about it.

They were very scared now. Christopher said, 'Because of you, I will get scolded and our pocket money will be just decreased if it is mom's wish.' Balish replied angrily, 'Hey! How are you saying that because of me this all is going to happen? Along with you, even I am going to get a big scolding. So shut your mouth up and prepare for the worst.' They went halfway fighting, when they saw their parents returning home in their car. At least they both didn't see their kids coming back home. They couldn't even say that- *Hey mom! We are here! See back, and pick us up too*. But they were in a situation where they couldn't do anything. They had to walk back home and obviously, they had to get a big scolding.

Mr. and Mrs. Laurence reached home. The home was silent and was filled with the sound of a cricket. They were happy for a moment, that their kids had slept, but it was totally the opposite! They were almost wriggling and twisting and finally reached home. They pressed the doorbell, with a great amount of fear.

The door opened. It was Mr. Laurence. He pulled Christopher and scolded Balish and closed the door. He called both of them in his room, which was filled with books and drinks. He knew only 3 things in life properly; Scolding, Reading, and Drinking. He scolded both of them equally.

It was midnight when the stubborn father left both of them and had mercy upon them. They both, with their heads down, went to sleep. Well, even if they had got scolding, they had a main achievement, to get to know about the secret that what was the reason due to which were beaten.

The next morning, both the children went school very sadly, as their friend Jack was departing. His flight was at 3 pm, and they went at 8 am to school. They had their last bell at 2:40 pm, and they decided that if they couldn't meet Jack at the dinner party, they will meet him at the airport, just before the aeroplane takes off.

They attended all the periods in the school and then they, with some more friends, went to the airport to see Jack. He waved his hands, as it was the time. Christopher and Balish quickly took some selfies with Jack and then he stepped onto the plane. Then there was no tension. Jack had gone. They had taken many selfies, and now Mrs. Polska told Jack that he can chat with his friends, and Christopher had his own phone, which his mother gifted him on his 10th birthday. After meeting Jack face to face maybe for the last time, they both went home. On their way, suddenly Balish noticed that there is a construction work going on in the forest, where Inferno Lord lives. He was stunned. How can anyone place a building in the dense forest? That too where the Inferno Lord lives? No, this can't happen. These types of questions and thoughts came in Balish's mind. He also started thinking that it was Inferno Lord who was going to live in this house which was ready to haunt the children. He had to stop it, for the sake of the lives of many children. He didn't want children to die for no reason.

They reached home. Mrs. Laurence was sitting on the carpet in her room and told the children to change and then come down. She had to talk to them. They both were scared. They had come to know why their mother had called them. She wanted to talk about the dinner's mayhem and the injuries and their connection with the injuries. As they knew, it was correct. Mrs. Laurence told them to sit down and she asked, 'Darlings, you must have got a great scolding by your father. But there is a reason, and you know the reason. So just, without any stammering, just tell the connection. Their body was shaking, as if some strong gush of cold chilly wind had pierced them. But Balish didn't tell lies. He quietly told, 'Mom, we dressed in an outfit, due to which we were beaten.

Mrs. Laurence became standstill. She said, 'That means...,'

'Yes mom, those were us who were wearing the outfit and we used our invisibility cloaks to be hidden until the dinner served, and then we would join the dinner line,' Christopher told in a quiet voice. Now her body also started shaking. She slapped them on the face and very angrily sent them out of the room. Now Balish was very confused. Why they were beaten? Why did their mom slap them? Why did the constructers start making a building in the dense forest? So many questions were overloaded in his mind. He had to find out; he was an extraordinary child, a normal wiz-person.

* * *

- CHAPTER -

4

The Construction

For the next few days, Balish's concentration on studies had gone down. He started finding out all the things that why all these things were happening in their surroundings. In the weekend, he told that he's going to play in the Quidditch ground, instead he went in the dense forest, after telling Christopher and Alfred the story and the trio entered the forest. Alfred and Christopher were very afraid of ghosts, though they didn't believe in ghosts.

But Inferno Lord was not a ghost; he was the god of the dark wizards. Dark wizards were those who served the Inferno Lord for a long time. It was believed that in the 19th century, the Inferno Lord was a normal man. He was wandering in the forest, when a massive earthquake came, the ground cracked, and the man had fallen in the crack. As per the mythology, that man is said to be Inferno Lord. 'But how he remained alive? How did he transform into a dark wizard lord?' Christopher asked Balish, who narrated the story of the Inferno Lord.

He replied, 'Guys, even I don't know the mystery of the Inferno Lord. Let's go a bit further in the forest,

so that we get any testimony or something related to that'.

Alfred said, 'Hey Balish, why are you doing this to put our lives on stake? I'm not going to join your party at all'!

On listening this, Balish said, 'If you want to go; then go. I don't want any doubtful or coward friends in my journey.'

Alfred couldn't say no to his best friend. So instead of saying no, he sighed and just walked quietly. They walked and walked, but no sign of testimony was to be seen. What was visible was only the ongoing-construction of building and trees and bushes. The trio was tired after walking so long. They reached until the edge of the forest, and the building was almost out of sight. They were not afraid now. Balish took out his water bottle and they drank water. Then they continued. When they couldn't find anything, they finally chose to go inside the ongoing construction of building and they hoped that they could find something as proof.

Alfred was shivering, but he couldn't show his expression, for Balish would be angry with him. He said, 'Balish, I know that you will save us if any trouble comes on us, but are you sure that this is safe'?

He said, 'Yes Alfred, of course it's safe. We'll just have a round of the building and then we'll come out. Nothing will happen to you, I guarantee it.' So Alfred and others entered. It was nothing but a hollow house until now. Balish was not scared at all, so he and his friends went up the staircase. Now came the point of being scared. They heard sounds of people in a room. And the sky also started becoming dark. Christopher and Alfred were really scared. Even Balish started sweating. But as he was the leader for now, he couldn't put a step back.

A sound came, 'Hey Polska, you are so rich. You must have a large amount of treasure and money. Please give it to me.' It wasn't the sound of Inferno Lord, for sure.

Balish and his friends went pale. 'Mr. Polska! Jack's father'! But didn't they go to Austria? As Christopher and Balish saw, Jack had stepped onto the plane and maybe their plane had also taken off until they reached home. But No! Some people had hijacked the plane! They were Inferno Lord's subjects, and as Mr. Polska was a rich businessman, they had kidnapped him for money.

Balish said, 'Friends, let's run home....'

Christopher said, 'For our lives'?

'No you dumbo, run home and quickly turn on your televisions. I'm dam sure that this hijacking news must be the breaking news for now,' Balish said.

And they did as Balish said. They ran out of the building quietly, and reached home. However they had to get a bit of scolding as they were late. It was 7 in the evening. But they didn't care. They just went to the T.V. room and saw the news. It was really the hijacking news.

The reporter was saying, 'A great incident here! A hijack of the plane AS-870! Many people have been kidnapped. This was appearing not a complete hijacking case, but rather a kidnapping case.

The trio didn't come to school the next day, as they had to investigate the building being constructed. They told their mothers that they're not feeling well. Christopher and Balish were still lying on their bed, under the blanket. They had opened their mini-laptops, which were of the size of a palm.

They were trying to find out any news related to hijacking. But the news was only saying that MANY people are kidnapped, rather than the specific news of the missing Polskas' family.

Balish whispered, and he couldn't say, otherwise Mrs. Laurence would come to check that everything was alright, 'Christopher, I think we should use our room window to run from here and start our investigation using my wand'.

Christopher said, in a bit high tone, 'Wow! Your magical wand has been repaired automatically. I didn't know about that.'

As we know, Balish had broken his wand during the journey to Jack's farewell party, so they both were helpless. They couldn't jump, as they won't be safe by doing that. So they finally decided to have patience.

A few days passed. Now the trio's drama of illness had vanished. They were ok. They continued going to school. However the exams were forthcoming and that was a great hurdle in their work.

But Balish didn't care. He didn't want to pass the exams. His main mission was to find out the mystery of Mr. Polska in the construction building and the strange echo. So for knowing more, he skipped lessons, especially the Potionology lessons, which were taught by Mrs. Exmas, a fat looking lady who always taught the children to experiment stupid, green-yellowish potions, and she just went stretching the lessons by telling everything about it. So these types of lessons were useless for the children, however they had to learn about it, as it would come in the exams.

Finally, the first exam came. It was of Sonic Studies. It was probably for wizards, including

Balish. Many questions would always come related to supersonic powers, which were generally useful only for wizards.

In the examination hall, Balish wasn't nervous. His concentration was not on the question paper. He just looked outside the windowpane, from where the part of forest's north edge was visible. However the building was very far.

Fredrick, at that time, was sneaking into other wizards' papers. His main work was to trouble Balish by his stupid spells, and to cheat in exams.

Unfortunately, for Fredrick, the headmaster, Mr. Morgan had spotted him during a round of the hall. He held him by the ear, without saying anything and threw him out of the hall. The other children became alert, leaving Balish. His attention was still on the forest's part.

Mr. Morgan was normally a gentle man, so he calmly asked Balish, 'Hey boy, where's your attention? Ok show your wand. I want to see something'.

As Balish's wand had broken, he said nothing but, 'Acosta!'

Acosta was a word that showed everything on its own. So the broken wand came up in the air and landed in Mr. Morgan's hand. He understood everything. He quietly said, 'Ok boy, you do your exam properly and you Fredrick, you come with me.'

Fredrick that day was severely punished. Balish quickly finished his exam and he ran when the bell rang. Christopher and Alfred asked Balish, 'Friend, how was your exam?', but Balish wasn't going to answer them. He just ran home, kept his bag and rushed towards the forest.

The trio was again ready to be in action. They re-entered the building after a few days. The walls were partly painted, and the base was ready. They went up to the stairs to scrutinize once more. This time there was no sound, but a strange yell came from the room, covering the whole house. It was Jack's!

The trio was deeply scared. What had happened to Jack? Balish wanted to just kick the room open and see what's going on there, but he had to be patient.

The truth was that Inferno Lord had been staying in that house for the last 2-3 days. And he had killed Mr. and Mrs. Polska and his main target was Jack now. Jack was yelling because he had seen Inferno Lord killing his parents in front of him, as they refused to give the Inferno Lord money.

Balish's patience came to an end. He kicked the room open and what he saw was unbelievable! Inferno Lord was laughing very loudly and peculiarly. He had finished Jack too. Christopher and Alfred saw his scary, frightening look and they ran from the spot. Inferno Lord and Balish were face-to-face now.

Remembering the past, he said, 'Hey, aren't you the same boy whose mother became my hunt and you escaped, no? It's good that you came on your own. Now your end is near. Be prepared for your DEATH! Hahahahaha'!

Balish couldn't defeat him at all this time at least. Firstly his wand had broken, and even if he could use his wand, Inferno' could use his special powers and finish Balish at once.

Balish once more ran for his life, but not being frightened, but to think of a way to defeat Inferno Lord.

At home, Christopher told all the story and his mother couldn't believe it, although it was the truth, and no one could differentiate it. Alfred also tried to tell his mother, but she didn't believe her child. How could anyone believe it though? It was a very rough and sad truth. The best friend of the friends, Jack was no more.

Even the reporters said not to show this stupid news. And however, Inferno' would have already ran away from his spot. Yes, he had run away very far, but the trio knew that he would surely return to kill Balish, for he was his greatest enemy right now. Balish had to be safe, and he would also think of a plan to kill Inferno Lord to save many lives.

Now the summer had disappeared. The winter holidays were forthcoming. The exams had finished and the results had also come out. Harold came up with 39 out of 40, the highest and Christopher, second top-scoring with 38 and a half. Balish was somewhere very down with only 23.

But he wasn't sad. When he hadn't learnt anything, then how could he get good marks?

* * *

- CHAPTER -

5

The Fun and Mystery in Disneyland

He forgot about the incident. Now, he wanted to enjoy the vacations. The Laurence family decided to go to Disneyland in California. It was their favorite place. They had booked the tickets, not by plane, but by train, as it was safer and more enjoyable.

They reached safely without any problem. On their first night, they decided to stay in a five star hotel. They ate lavish food, slept on a fluffy, soft mattress and enjoyed a lot, including the luxury and surroundings of the hotel.

Next day Christopher said, 'Hey Balish, let's go in the snow. It's too fun. Come bro.' Balish loved snow, but he hated cold. He hated the coldness every day that always pinched Balish's body every morning when he got up. So he refused. Now Christopher got angry with Balish and he didn't talk to him for a long period of time. It was a very fussy thing on which Christopher got angry. However, Mr. and Mrs. Laurence were enjoying a lot. They stayed in the sun whenever it appeared, and the hot sun always took away the coldness which they hated. Balish also often went and sat with them to enjoy the sunny days.

After staying 3 days in hotel, it was time for them to go to their next destination - Disneyland! Balish was the most keyed up whereas Christopher was angry and he wasn't talking to anyone.

They were going in the famous BMW car with the help of Mr. Laurence's friend. Balish was ready for meeting all the Disney characters, from Mickey Mouse to Pikachu. Christopher wasn't too excited, though he was also happy that his dreams would become true.

When they reached the gate, Balish said, 'Whoooo daddy, what a place this is. I used to read about it in newspapers and watch in television, but today I'm gonna meet all the Disney characters'.

Mr. Laurence laughed and said, 'Where is the fun in watching or reading, let's see them in real'.

Christopher had to be happy and energetic, whereas he was just sighing time-to-time and ignoring his dad's words. Then only his mother came near him with a smiling face and said, 'Darling, what happened? Why are you so quiet? Come, we're about to enter the dreamland - Disneyland! Cheer up Christopher.'

He said, 'Mom, should I tell the truth, I wanted to stay at home. Here there is no one to play with me. I know that I am a big boy now, but still for fun....'

Balish came and said, 'Oh come on bro. Sorry I didn't play with you so what happened? We have 20 more days. We will have a lot of fun. Don't worry.' On hearing the kind words from Balish, Christopher said, 'I'm also sorry bro. I am grateful that I have got a great brother like you.' 'Ok, Ok, now if your emotional talk has finished, shall we enter or will we stay outside only', Dad said. Then they all laughed and went inside.

The Disneyland they always saw in newspapers and advertisements. The real Disneyland was very different from that. It was like a dream. Every stone had different colors on the roads, the castle of Disneyland had many lighting colors shining and changing on its walls. It was as if they were the chief guest of a special program.

Balish suddenly spotted something strange. A person hid his face by a mask very peculiarly and was rushing towards his car as if it was his last moment. What could it be? Balish, anyhow, had to find out the mystery of everything. But he couldn't understand how to catch him. Ah yes! He noted the number of the car with the help of a stick on the snowy road. Then he quickly took a quill and a parchment and noted it down.

After having a lot of fun in Disneyland, it was time for Balish to find out the mystery of the running away masked person. However, he wasn't a detective; he had to at least find out about this mystery man.

Balish was thinking too much about the masked-man and started remaining in deep thoughts. Seeing the changing behavior of Balish, Mrs. Laurence was upset and one day she held him and said, 'Balish my son, I've noticed that you are a bit tensed these days. You should have enjoyed this opportunity, however you are doing some work secretly. Now tell your mom what happened.' He was helpless now. How could he hide something from his own mom? He said, in a bit stammering way, 'Mom, I.... I am v....very confused. A man was r.....running away, may be for a peculiar r... reason. I don't know w...why but I want t....to find out the secret,' and now a bit confidently, 'Mom, I promise you that this will be my last investigation and then I will never..... Never do any type of investigation or something related to this'. She said happily and tapping Balish on the back, 'Now that's my boy. Come, enjoy the snow.'

Christopher threw a snowball on mom and laughed, 'Hahahahaha mom, lol!' She also replied by throwing a snowball. Balish turned his face around and closed his eyes for some time. He remembered the moments when he lost his mother and how Christopher's mother adopted him without any hesitation. Tears rolled down from his cheeks. He wanted to thank Mrs. Laurence, but how? She would always do something that Balish would feel extra grateful.

Another 16 days passed like a gush of wind. Now it was time to say goodbye to California and, especially Disneyland. These opportunities came just because of kindness of Mr. and Mrs. Laurence. They were very kind.

While coming back, in the train, Christopher said, 'Hmmmm, so these days have passed so fast. I just loved Disneyland. Wow! What a place it was. It is probably one of the most famous and extraordinary places on our Earth. Hey Balish, did you enjoy'?

'Yes, why wouldn't I enjoy. It was really brilliant', Balish said, but hiding his sorrow. He wanted to find out the mystery of the running man, in which he failed. But the chances had not gone to zero. He took out his parchment and saw the noted plate number. It was of California's cars, but he could repair his wand and go Disneyland secretly one day by finding out whose car was that. Yes, it was a great idea. At home, when he reached, he relaxed and then he took out his mini-laptop and came to know about the plate number. It was of a man named Mr. Loppy. He appeared to be from a middle-class family. However, Balish had to find out the mystery.

He had saved his pocket money since the last year, and he had collected 96 Euros. The wand mending needed 80 Euros, which means only 16 Euros would be left with Balish. But he didn't care. He wanted to be successful in his LAST mission, as he promised to Mrs. Laurence.

The very next day, in the darkness of the night, Balish slipped out of his bed and flew through the window using his repaired wand. He was very excited, not for re-visiting Disneyland, but for finding out the mystery. But he had to be quick, because if he would be late, Mrs. Laurence would be worried.

He reached at 6 in the morning. He saw the same roads, filled with colorful pebbles of green, yellow and red etc. He went to the nearby Transport Department and enquired about the man, Mr. Loppy, whose car number Balish had noted down. The receptionist gave the information, and Balish did not waste any time. Within two hours, he had to return at any cost. He found the house somehow too, and in 1 hour, he was outside the house. The house was situated in a very narrow road, and cracks were visible on the outer walls of the house. It wasn't looking a newly built house, it was an old house.

Old or new, it did not matter to Balish. His main mission was to find out the mystery. He saw the same car parked behind the house. He opened the door, and he heard the voice of a man. He was saying to someone else, 'Hey bro, I managed to steal some gold money in the last few days, but be careful that no one should notice us'. He wasn't aware that Balish was already noticing him. The second voice was also heard, saying- 'No ways! Not even the police can find out our secret place, until they find out the plate number of our car, which is impossible to be found.' Balish was very excited to catch the thieves. Thank God he had brought his mini-laptop, and he quickly called the police.

In no time, the police reached and their siren was taciturn so that the thieves were not alert. Policemen went upstairs, opened the door and while pointing their guns to the gang of thieves, said, 'You're busted'! Now the gang couldn't even run away. There was no window to escape. They were finally caught, and Balish smiled. Suddenly he noticed the time and he had already spent three-fourth time, that's quarter to 8. He had to rush, and he quickly took out his wand, and flew away from the spot before the police could shake hands with the master!

He increased the speed, not thinking about the rules that wizards couldn't ride on their brooms over 180 km per hrs. And Balish had toppled 200 km. But it was office time in Balish's city, so no one had noticed him. He safely reached home and on his bed back. He was just in time. Mrs. Laurence was climbing up the stairs to open the window curtains. After doing so, she let Balish and Christopher wake up to be ready.

Christopher said, 'Ready... for what? Are we going somewhere today too'?

'Yes darling', Mrs. Laurence said in her calm voice, 'we're going to the wizardry fair today, where many games would be played and prizes would be given away. But don't worry Christopher; you can also participate in this fair. No one will restrict you'. Balish had attended this fair once with Mrs. Lane, just a week before she became the hunt of Inferno Lord. He again cried. Christopher knew it and said, 'Oh Balish, you become emotional so easily. Now, my mom is your mom too. Forget the past and think about the future. It will be so fun. And you remember its Christmas Eve today. Tomorrow is Christmas Balish! Wow, so much fun in the winter holidays'.

But Balish couldn't forget it. He had to take vengeance. Suddenly Mrs. Laurence broke his sadness and said, 'Christopher! Don't forget that your holidays are finishing after just 2 days'!

'Hahaha mom, chill. Let us enjoy these 2 days at least', Christopher said and Balish laughed.

They got ready to go to the fair. Balish didn't know that he's gonna get the bravery award for catching the gang today only.

At the fair, many wiz-friends of Balish came. Just then, Balish saw Fredrick. He had bought a new wand and a spell-brewing machine, and Balish knew that he's gonna experiment them on him only, and he had to prepare himself. But he didn't worry, he enjoyed the fair. The award distribution was at the last, to maintain the suspense. Before that, there was a wizard talent show too; however Balish intentionally didn't submit his name for participation. Many wizards had shown many experiments and stunts too, even Fredrick tried his best, but his flop things continued.

Now was the time for the award distribution. There were many veteran wiz-judges to find out who did the bravest thing by scanning their minds with the help of supersonic powers. This was the highlight of the prize distribution. One judge shouted, 'Ladies and gentlemen, welcome to the annual wizard fair! I know some children, especially from the SuperSonics', must be enjoying the winter vacations. We all know that Christmas is just tomorrow, and whosoever is going to win the award, the award is going to be the gift for Christmas. I hope that you must have done a lot of bravery to win the award. Great deeds wizards'! The wizards who truly showed their bravery were shouting, but Balish, who did the bravest work, wasn't excited. He instead went to shops and just saw the attractive items.

The main judge was Mr. Abner, the head of the W.C.M (Wizard Competitions Ministry). He had a long face, with a black moustache and curly hair. As he had a great post, he was going to give the prize to the winners. Before giving the prizes, he said, 'I'm very fortunate to get a chance to give away the prize to the bravest wizard. I will be very happy to meet the wizard who has shown his courage to fight the best, thank you.'

The wizards cheered and clapped for Mr. Abner, except Balish, who had already bought a miniature statue of his favorite Quidditch player, Iron Layshout of Australia which cost only 6 Euros. The judges saw each other, nodded their heads and started their powers.

The sky became green for a moment and returned to its normal colour. Then Mr. Beatstrich, another judge said, 'It's done! We have the results with us. Are you ready wizards'? The wizards cheered again, and Mr. Beatstrich started announcing the results, 'The third position goes to George of Oxford Wizards Institute'!

George came up to the stage and thanked Mr. Abner. It was a great feeling to shake hands with the head of competitions of wizards. After a moment, there was silence again. They were desperate to know the 2nd bravest wizard. Mr. Beatstrich continued, 'The second position goes to... Danny of SuperSonics'!

The crowd cheered 'Danny! Danny!' and Balish heard it. He was happy to know that someone else is also brave in his school. His stepping on the stage was very clear and audible. 'Ok, OK', said Mr. Beatstrich, as he was going to announce the winner of the bravery award. He shouted, 'so ladies and gentlemen, the bravest wizard of this city is........'

"Bravest wizard of the year"

The crowd was silent. Balish sighed and kept seeing the statue he bought.

'Balish Lane of SuperSonics'!!!! Said Mr. Beatstrich.

Balish, Christopher and Mr. - Mrs. Laurence were awestruck. They couldn't believe their ears.

Suddenly Mr. Beatstrich said again, 'Is master Balish present here'?

'Yes, Mr. Beatstrich', said Balish, as he ran towards the stage. Just as Mr. Abner saw him, he went into another world. He just thought and he came to know all about the life of Balish. He shook hands with a child who was appearing more famous than him. He said, 'Oh my!!! What a child he is! Thanks young man for showing your bravery. I'm very proud to give this award to you'.

The crowd clapped, together with Fredrick, who couldn't believe it. 'How can Balish get the bravery award? Oh, if it's like that, then my experiments will be a flop in front of him. I won't do that', he whispered to himself. The crowd was still clapping for Balish and cheering him.

At home, Mrs. Laurence hugged Balish so tightly that he couldn't breathe properly. She said, 'Oh my boy, we are very proud of you. You're so extraordinary, I didn't know! I'm really proud of you. Keep it up'. Christopher wasn't jealous, but happy that his friend had done a great job. But Mr. Laurence said, 'What did he do? Did he stop a tsunami? Did he manage to go to the core of the Earth or the sea? I don't understand'.

Mrs. Laurence replied, 'Oh honey! So what? How can the judge misjudge the wiz-children? He must have done something that he got the first place. Go Balish and Christopher, take rest in your room. You must be tired'. 'Oh yes mom, I'm really tired', said Christopher. Just then Balish laughed and said, 'Oh Christopher! You're saying as if only you are tired. Even I'm very tired, let's go'.

* * *

- CHAPTER -

6

Mora Leka

That day Christopher didn't get up from bed until 6 in the evening, when he slept in the afternoon and that too when Mrs. Laurence called them for supper, 'Balish and Christopher, do you have any idea that you both are sleeping since 12?

Christopher replied, 'Yeah mom, we're coming, just a minute'.

Just as he saw on his right side, Balish wasn't there; instead he had gone to play with his friends Alfred and Mora Leka, a newly-shifted child. He was also in his first-year, as he was 12 years old. They talked and came to know that Mora is also a normal wiz-person like Balish. They were astonished. That meant that Mora is also an extraordinary child like Balish.

Balish happily jumped with laughter, 'Yeah! At least there is someone who's like me. Now I can't be lonely. Thanks Mora'.

Mora also smiled and said, 'Balish, that means that we can play in both of the school grounds (the normal and the Quidditch one). I'm really excited to go to school!'. Then they decided to play Quidditch in the school ground. It was allowed to play during holidays, but you have to show your robes and your wand, on which the badge of SuperSonics' was visible. In view of the fact that Mora was new, Balish would introduce him to the guards.

They reached, and the guard Mr. Kahayan recognized Balish and Alfred, as they always met him in the lunch break, but not Mora. He gently wished Balish, 'Oh hi! How are you? Meeting you after a long time. Don't worry; your school is opening just after 2 days. By the way, who's this lovely guy? Is he new or what'? Balish laughed, 'Yes Mr. Kahayan, he is Mora Leka. Like me he's also a normal wiz-person. He's gonna join the school subsequent to the holidays'.

Mr. Kahayan smoothened his long beard and winked to Balish, 'Oh never mind boy. Welcome Mora. This school is good, but be very careful of the teachers, they're very strict'! Balish just pushed Mora, 'Oh Mr. Kahayan! We have come to play Quidditch. We will talk to you later on. See yah'! They played till 7, until Christopher approached and Mr. Kahayan recognized him too, 'Hi Christopher. Your friends are playing Quidditch, with a new friend. Go boy'.

Christopher said to himself, 'New friend? Let's see'.

When Christopher stepped onto the ground, Mora's eyes noticed Christopher and called him. 'Oh hi friend, what's your name? Where are Balish and Alfred '? Christopher asked.

Mora replied with a smile on his brownish face- 'Oh hi. My name is Mora Leka. I have recently shifted to this city. It's a great ground. However, your friends are fetching water from the nearby drinking water pump. They must be coming. Hey, they have come'. Christopher ignored Mora and Alfred and pulled Balish by the hand, 'Hey Balish, mom is finding you. Come home quickly'! Balish said, 'Ok then see you tomorrow or maybe straight after the vacations. After all, it's a matter of just 2 days'. They waved hands to each other as Alfred and Mora also went home.

As soon as Balish entered, Mrs. Laurence said in a worried tone, 'Oh Balish, how can you go to play without having your supper and milk? You know, I was so worried. Now come and have your supper'.

Balish sighed as he ate his supper discussing with his mother, 'You know mom, a new child has come in the city. We are friends now and the best thing is that Mora is also a normal wiz-person. I'm very happy mom, Yippee!

Suddenly Balish realizes that today is the Quidditch final and he said, 'Oh, today is the Quidditch final between Australia and France; I can't miss that, I'm gonna watch that mom'.

Before Mrs. Laurence could say something, Balish had run upstairs to watch his match. Between the match, the doorbell rang. It was Mora. Balish was surprised. How did he find out his home? Even Alfred wasn't there. Mora said, 'Hey Balish, I wanted your parchments on which you have done your work. I had to copy them. But don't worry. I'll give them before the vacations are over'.

Balish was annoyed that Mora came during his favorite match, now he had to open his trunk and find it from the stack of parchments and a box of quills. But he kept his anger under control and quietly opened his trunk and took out the copies and gave them to Mora and ran upstairs before Mora could even say thanks to him. Mrs. Laurence laughed and said to Mora, 'Never mind my boy. His nature is like that only. So just leave the matter'. Mora winked and while leaving, he said- 'Oh no Mrs. Laurence. I never mind'.

During the last 5 minutes of the match, it was Australia reeling with only 31 points, whereas France had reached 52. Balish turned the television off and quietly ate dinner without answering anyone. He stamped his foot while going to sleep upstairs, and in his room, he saw a creature which was much related to Balish. It was none other than Iogy, his pet pigeon, who had turned the television on. Balish didn't notice the breaking news but Iogy. He shouted, 'Iogy! You're back! Oh, I was so worried about you. I just missed you to a great extent'.

Iogy told in a sign language that Balish should look at the breaking news. The reporter was saying in a loud tone, ***'Australia, the defending champs, have succeeded in defending their title by defeating France by 58-56. Yes, you may have turned your televisions off when Australia was almost succumbing to their arch-rivals, but a miracle happened. Michael Grey, the Striker, just kept scoring for his team in the last 4 minutes'***.

Balish couldn't believe it. How could Michael Grey become the Striker? He was the substitute, so that means that....... Iron Layshout was substituted! Balish was very angry, that what did the coach do? Even if his team won, he wanted Iron to be the hero, not Michael. He knew the address of the Quidditch stadium and it wasn't time. The presentation must be going on. He rushed using his wand.

In the midway, Alfred saw him. He shouted, 'Hey Balish! Where are you going at night? Do yah have any intention of doing any investigation? Wait, I'm also coming'. But Balish ignored him and kept going. Alfred was flabbergasted.

He reached the stadium, hammering the guards standing there. He ran and finally reached the place where the presentation was going on. He shouted, 'Stop this dim-witted presentation. Coach, do you reckon what you've done? You have affronted my player, Iron Layshout. Balish lost his control and was just arguing with the coach. Balish also said, ask for clemency right now or else I'll......'

The coach, who was standing there, wasn't angry. Instead he smirked and patted Balish on the shoulder, 'Oh my boy. What happened if I substituted Iron? Our team has won man, but if you really want me to ask for clemency, then ok. I'll right away say sorry to Iron'. He ordered the physio to call Iron. Balish didn't know, but Iron was injured.

He saw Iron. He had met him once in his early-age, as Mrs. Lane had told him. He was cramping and walking with his hands over his leg. His broomstick was broken and the 2 physio were carrying him on their shoulders. Balish realized everything. He told the Coach, 'Sorry coach, but I didn't know the matter. I instead turned the T.V. off when Australia was lurching by 21 points'.

Coach, with his blue eyes, blinked and said, 'No probs. It was a misinterpretation, which is now cleared. Balish sighed and was ready to return. But at home, Mr. Laurence was looking *Moon Quidditch*, which was the channel where international Quidditch matches were telecasted. He boiled with anger when looked Balish's drama. He called Christopher and asked him angrily, 'Christopher, how can you be so negligent? Do you know what a great slur is going to happen because of Balish? Can't you stop him ever from going outside anytime and especially for the acts like this'?

Christopher, with his heads down grumbled to himself, 'Let Balish come. I'm not going to leave him'. Balish was returning home, with an autograph in his hand of the Coach and a cheerful face through the window when he spotted Iogy. He said, 'Hi Iogy! See,

I've got the autograph of the newly-made Australian coach, but I forgot to ask his name'.

But Iogy moved to the left and behind her appeared Mr. Laurence. Suddenly Balish's cheerful face turned into a frowned smile, 'Uh oh'? Mr. Laurence welcomed him inside with extreme anger, but with a calm face. 'Come Balish. Welcome back'. Balish said fretfully, 'D......Dad. You.... Here? I... I mean it's too....too late no'?

Mr. Laurence said, 'That's what I'M going to ask you. Why were you outside so late? Didn't you think what your father would do with you? Do you realize what the time is? It's 11:30 pm! And what did you think that I'm not gonna come to know about the drama you created at the stadium? You've put my head down'.

Behind Mr. Laurence, niggling through the door, Christopher was laughing quietly, showing his expressions to Balish. He noticed him, but he couldn't tell Dad that Christopher is laughing. He was really angry with him. To Balish's luck, Mrs. Laurence came to the rescue. She pushed Christopher from the front and confronted his husband.

'Hubby, leave the poor boy. It's too late, let's go to bed, and Balish', winking to him from the back, 'you too go back to bed. It's too late'. 'Yah mom, don't fret. I'll sleep right away. I'm sorry dad', Balish apologized.

Mr. Laurence said in a grumpy voice, 'Ok Ok, today your mom has saved you, but commit to memory that even if you dream of going outside the home at such a time, you'll not be safe next time'. 'Good night dad and mom. See you tomorrow', Balish said in a reassured voice.

The holidays were finally over, and it was time for Balish to return to the torrent of supersonical powers and physics, the complicated subjects. At the first day of the new semester, Mr. Jorge arrived in the class. The children wished them, 'Good morning sir'. Mr. Jorge instead of telling them to sit down just showed his hand and put it down. The children understood and they sat down. He said,

'My dear children, I hope that many of you must have enjoyed your holidays. Wasn't it fun guys'? Many 'YES' came from the class. Then Mr. Jorge cleared his throat and said,

'So children, you must have also done your holiday homework. Show me your parchments. I'll give grades according to that'.

Balish said to himself and maybe to his partner, Mora, 'Oops, I just forgot that. My homework is incomplete'. As he was in trouble, Mora took out his wand and pointed it to Mr. Jorge and whispered,

'Leistacio'. Mr. Jorge froze as if taken out of the freezer. Everyone was silent. As Mora had whispered, no one had a qualm that Mora is responsible. Actually, the effect of this freezing-spell was for 1 day, but as Mora had upgraded his wand, hence the effect now was for 2 days.

Balish happily said in thoughts, 'Yes'!

Mora murmured to Balish, 'Thank me bro. I have saved you. If I wouldn't be here, then you imagine what the strictest teacher would have done to you'.

Balish shook hands with Mora while going back home and told Christopher all the truth. He laughed, 'Whoa man! What an exertion you have done! But yes, keep in mind that mom should not come to know about....... t..... this'....

Mrs. Laurence was standing just behind them. Christopher noticed her through Balish's shining glasses. Balish could not complete the sentence,

'That Mora helped me in impeding Mr. Jorge from looking our incomplete parchments'.

Mrs. Laurence clapped, 'Oh! So that's the matter. Very cleverly you fooled your teacher. Great'! Now Balish also left a grimace, and said, 'Chill mom. Don't worry. The upshot will certainly finish after 2 days. And my homework will also finish. Don't worry'.

She also left a long grin and irately said, 'If I receive any complaint from any teacher, I'll be the nastiest. I am warning you Balish... and sparing you, but not next time'.

At supper, Balish didn't appear. He was doing his incomplete homework, because of which he almost got an admonishment by Mrs. Laurence. From downstairs, Christopher shouted. 'Balish, come down for supper. Your milk and quiche are getting cold. Come fast. We'll eat together.

He had no intention to have his supper, which was semi-cold now. He came outside the room and groaned, 'No, Chris. I will first finish my homework. It's just the spell naming and their effects. Maybe I may come for dinner. If not, then you can bring my plate of food in my room'.

'Ok as you wish'. Christopher said.

He had finished all the work up to the last 3 spells, which were most difficult to explain. Out of them, one was used by the Inferno Lord (The Conflagration spell). It was judged as the official spell for the rarely known dark wizards and witches, which meant that only dark wiz-witches could use them. During writing the definition of the Conflagration spell, he remembered the occurrence once again. His scratch started itching. Iogy came and put one of the strongest liniments for scratches. Balish was screaming-'Aaaaah! That burns, Iogy. Put it less'.

Tears were rolling down on his cheeks because he was missing his mother a lot. Iogy patted his shoulder. His soft feathers gave a great feeling to Balish. Soon it was time for dinner. His homework was finished. He sighed and went down. The dining table was empty. Christopher had gone out to play and Mrs. Laurence was preparing food in the kitchen. She noticed Balish and said tranquilly, 'Welcome Balish. Finished your homework finally'?

'Yes mom. Can I go outside to play', Balish hesitantly asked, despite the fact that he knew that Mrs. Laurence would say NO. But Mrs. Laurence overlooked him and prepared dinner. Balish didn't mind because she had to say no. Christopher was returning home, saying bye to his friend Alfred. He saw Iogy. He hadn't seen her for the past 2 days, so he hugged her tightly and with great astonishment he said,

'Hi Iogy, it's a long period of time since we met last time. I think at least 5 years have passed. I just missed you a lot. Now you aren't going anywhere ok'?

Iogy made a noice and said 'yes' in her lingo-Anotrench. It was the bureaucrat language of the animals of wizard society. The dinner was served by Mrs. Laurence. Her husband has also come from office. It was a heavy schedule today for him. He said, 'Honey, first of all you serve us dinner. We're very hungry'. Iogy with her feet tapped the base of the perch to show that she also wants food. Christopher and Balish also snapped their plates with their spoons and asked for food. They had a lovely dinner that day. The complete family was having dinner together.

Abruptly in Balish's dream that night, he saw something very unusual. He saw the Australian Quidditch coach standing beside Mora Leka. He heard him mumbling to Mora, 'My boy, this secret should remain a secret. No one should come to know that you're my.......' Balish murmured in his sleep, 'My what? Tell Mora, what is your relation with the sassy Australian coach? I want to know'. The moment he was about to know what Mora was speaking, his sleep was interrupted by a flock of pigeons. Several pigeons whooshed into Balish's room. Iogy shrieked. Balish woke up with sweat oozing from his face, as he had to know the secret. The pigeons dropped many letters on Balish's coverlet. Christopher also got up and nearly squealed when Balish covered his mouth.

'No Christopher. Mom will get up and get surprised by these pigeons. Calm down, I'll tell the matter'. Christopher took some seconds to settle down, and then the pigeons had also flown away and disappeared in the darkness. 'Will yah help me Christopher in opening and reading these letters'? 'Of course, I'll turn on the mini-top torch. You don't worry bro, Christopher smiled and said.

They opened the letters one by one. The first letter was from Alfred. He wrote,

Dear Balish,

I think there is a connection between Mora Leka and the Australian Coach. I don't really know, but yes. I think we should find out the matter.

Now Balish was in a great dilemma. He promised Mrs. Laurence that he would never investigate ever. But as this was a secret, he had to find the connection. All the letters were same. The same message was written.

The next day while going to school, Balish saw the construction going on and he noticed that there were many cracks on the walls when he went a bit near to it. The construction team was also nowhere seen. But Balish didn't care. He wanted to know about the sassy coach and Mora's relationship.

Christopher was sleepy. He spent at least 2 hours in keeping the letters in a box to keep the secret with them only. He grinned and said, 'Hey Balish, I don't think that investigating this silly topic is useful. What happened if Mora is Mr. Jimmy's relative? What do we have to do with their personal problems'?

Balish said in a low tone, 'friend, investigating is our work. I just love doing these types of things. So just keep investigating'.

Christopher wished to reply, but could not and said to himself, 'I shouldn't argue with this helpless boy. Mummy will scold him and I will not be a part of it.'

Hmmm, Balish, I don't want to join your party. You do it on your own, or take help from Alfred. I would not insist him to leave the party'.

Balish nodded and went to school. Mora that day was absent. He had severe fever and cold and that was the reason that he didn't come to school.

Balish and Christopher were surprised. Mora was absent! They had to ask him for the relationship, but unfortunately it wasn't their day. They however had Mora's mini-top number, and they had to ask him through mini-tops, that too when he's alone at home.

They tolerated all the studies and finally the bell rang. All the wizards ran home. There were separate bells for wizards and for normal non-wizard students. But as Balish was a normal wiz-person, he also ran along the wizards. He rushed home, threw his cauldron and trunk, took a quill and a parchment and called Alfred for the thing called investigation.

Alfred rang the bell and Christopher opened the door. He wasn't excited, as he wasn't in the group. Only Balish and Alfred were interested in these types of things.

They both went into their rooms and took out their mini-laptops. They tried to find out the full name of Mr. Jimmy, the Australian coach through many wiz-sites. But nothing was there which could be useful to Balish and Alfred. Only Mr. Jimmy was the name.

Next, after thinking, Balish whispered to Alfred with his eyebrows curved downwards and his eyes ignoring Christopher,

'I think that there's no connection, however we won't leave doing the investigation'.

Just then Mrs. Laurence opened the door. She had gone to the market to buy groceries for the dinner. There, Alfred 's shoes were lying upside down. She was astonished that who's come here. There were already two shoes in the rack, then who? She went upstairs, tiptoeing.

Balish was just holding his wand when it shuddered. It was giving a signal. Oh no! mom is coming upstairs. Balish quickly whispered to Alfred,

'Run! Mom is coming up! Take my wand and hide somewhere below the windowpane. Quickly! Rush'!

Christopher sighed. Mrs. Laurence was already halfway up. Alfred murmured,

'You Dumbo Balish! Don't you know we can use the freezing charm instead of just rushing'?

'But what'll happen you know, mom will freeze for a day. Thank God I've never thought to upgrade my charm'.

So Alfred held the wand, which expanded into a broom. He flew and hid in Mrs. Laurence's room by flying.

The door opened. Mrs. Laurence was standing like a curious woman. She saw Balish with his mini-top. She had warned Balish to investigate ever, and Balish's truth had plopped like a water drop in a glass.

She shouted, 'Balish! You had promised me that you'll never investigate, so what's this? This mini-top... this mini-top should've been out of home until now. So now just kick this thing out or else nothing will be worse than ME'!

Alfred heard all the matter and he rushed quickly, just beside Balish's room. As soon as Balish threw it with a frowned face, Alfred caught it. Balish quietly left the room and Christopher also left a frowning smile.

'N...No mom! I'...I'm not involved in this fussy thing! You can...'

'Stop! As if I don't know your work'!

Christopher wanted to shout at his mom, but he didn't do so. He stamped his feet and banged the door behind Mrs. Laurence, who was stunned.

Outside home, Alfred was giggling in the garden. Balish was sobbing and going somewhere. Alfred followed him and after a distance, he kept his hands over his shoulders.

He turned behind and he saw his companion holding his laptop. He was really happy to see this. He hugged Alfred and said, 'Oh my friend! I'm so grateful to you. If you had not been there, my mini-laptop would have been...'

'SSSHHH! do not say all these. A friend in need is a friend indeed', said Alfred.

The next day Mora came. Balish and Alfred were ready now. They had to find out now. In their games period, Balish pulled Mora and they sat on the spectator's bench in the Quidditch stadium.

'I want to play Balish, my friend. Leave me alone', said Mora.

'Not so easily my friend! First I'll ask you some questions. You answer 'em correctly and I'll leave you', giggled Balish.

'Ok ok! Then ask fast'!

'First of all, who is Mr. Jimmy'?

'M.... Mr. Jimmy? Who...Who Mr. Jimmy', Mora stammered.

'That's what' I'm asking. Answer or else I'll ask Mr. Jimmy himself'.

'Ok.... Ok! I'm telling. He's my...'

'He's my FATHER'! Said Mora, 'Mr. Jimmy is my father so what'?

'What! Shouted Balish with a wide mouth and eyes.

He was astonished. Mr. Jimmy - his father! Mora could be so famous, but no one knew. Just then the bell rang. It was time to continue and the wizards went to their respective classes.

* * *

- CHAPTER -

7

The Quidditch League

Balish and Alfred were wonderstruck. Their mission was complete. They wanted to find the secret out, in which they succeeded. Christopher was jealous now. He came to know that Alfred caught the mini-laptop when Balish threw it on Mrs. Laurence's order.

When they were returning from school gossiping, Balish laughed and hi-fived Alfred in front of Christopher.

'Whoa man! What an experience it was! I just loved your catch Alfred. I didn't know you're such a good catcher'.

'Nah nah, it was just a fussy little catch. I can do thousands of catches like that'. Christopher lowered his eyes and with his hands in a punching position, he went home.

'Mom, they have succeeded', said Christopher in a rough voice.

'In what'?

'In investigating once more'!

'Oh my god! These children of this century! I don't know what fun do they get in doing these types of things, and soon they will be in the newspapers named, 'Mr. Detective Balish!' Let him come, I'll talk to him'.

Christopher giggled and went in his room, with jealousy still for Balish.

'Really? Ok bye, see yah', said Alfred in the middle of the gossip. They reached home. Just as he opened the main door, Mrs. Laurence was in a fake smile. She had worn her apron until now, as she was finishing her house chores, which were almost done. She was ready to scold him, maybe.

'Uh um, mom. So I think you must be ready to scold me, as I'm sure that Christopher might have told the truth ruthlessly no? But no problem. You know what? Mora Leka, my friend, is the son of the newly elected Australian Quidditch coach, Jimmy Leka. What a news no? Like that, even his friends can also be stars', Balish said with full confidence.

Mrs. Laurence, after hearing this sentence, forgot her anger and went in her room, sighing. She was neither angry nor happy. She wanted her children to stay happy, and Balish was. Christopher didn't come for supper that day. He was also searching for a work of investigation in the city, so that he may also get some praise from his mom.

He searched and searched and found a 'WANTED' sign. There was a thief in the loose. Reporters and many police officers have surrounded that place. They were asking some questions. Christopher didn't find any interest in that and after an hour of failure searching, he gave up hope.

'It's a great sunny day my wiz-children, said Mr. Hulhuge the headmaster.

'Yes sir', yelled the children with full hope that Mr. Hulhuge would say something new, and it wasn't new, but energizing.

'So my children, we all know that annually we organize the Inter-House Quidditch Cup. But... this time we are going to organize an Inter-SCHOOL Quidditch League'!

'Yeah, Yippee, Whooooo', were the excited calls and yells of the happy children.

'I'm very happy too my kids ! Now I'm going to call out the names of the schools who will participate in the League'.

There was silence in the assembly. The curious children were eager to know the schools.

'First of all- our Supersonics' school of Wiz-Witchcraftdry, secondly the Yugados Institute of Starting Quidditch. And children be are careful of this school particularly. The coach of this Institute has reached international levels. Thirdly we have the Walkrys' school. The thing about this school is that they have come straight from Africa. As we all know, Quidditch is the famous wizard sport of some countries in Africa, so don't take both the schools lightly. And yes.... Don't forget the most experienced Quidditch School of our city... I am sure that you know that'.

'Oh yes sir, said the children silently, 'it's none other than the Quiddos School of Pro Quidditch League. This school has hosted many leagues, so the 3 schools are shortlisted to be very careful.

'I expected this sentence my energetic boys and girls. So I'm announcing the date. As per our decision, the date has been scheduled for 3rd October this year. I hope that we have many days for training. Ok, silence youngsters. Today is a special day too. I will introduce you to our coach until the league. Meet Mr. Jimmy Leka, the coach of The International Australian Quidditch Team'!

'What! Yeah, Yippee'! Shouted the children.

Balish and Alfred were awestruck the most. They couldn't believe their eyes & ears. It was the sassy coach. And now this sassiness was about to be increased because probably now the league was in his safe hands.

'Whoa', whispered Christopher to himself. His mood became very happy when he heard the announcement of Mr. Jimmy as the Quidditch coach of their school. It was a special occasion for the wizards.

'Attention'! Said Mr. Hulhuge, 'for participating in this competition, ONLY WIZARDS ARE ELIGIBLE AS EVER. The rules won't change. There will be a pot in the air for confirming that only wizards reach the height, and they would put their information. From those names, we will test their abilities and the top 11 will be selected for the starting XI. The other 4 top wizards will be kept as substitutes. I hope you have understood. Thank you and have a good day !'.

He smiled and departed. There was excitement, but only in the wizards. What was the fault of the normal children? What would they do? The children were sad. They didn't know Quidditch, though they would try in their Games period. But at least they should get a chance for themselves. They wanted to have a meeting once before the league, and very quickly.

Fredrick was whistling as he was going to put his name for the league in the pot when Balish ran and passed by him. Fredrick got annoyed and grinned.

'Oh Balish! Howzat? Putting your failure name for your failure performance boy? You aren't capable of this competition. Go and study'.

Balish instead of getting angry, just laughed and said,

'I'm getting pity on you my friend. I think that whatever you have said just a while ago is same to you. You study and improve yourself'.

He took his wand and shouted,

'Westo'!

The parchment of information flew on its own and landed in the wiggling pot which was already filled half. Fredrick also flew with the help of his old, rusty broom, which was gifted by his father, Mr. Alwoy when he and Mrs. Alwoy were departing to Sweden for their postings.

Fake tears rolled down from Fredrick's cheeks.

'Xsendtre 800, Polish company, max speed of 150 km/h. Hope my luck gives support to me'.

Balish giggled and went back to his class for lunch.

Mr. Kahayan was standing there. He saw Balish as if he wanted to just hug him tightly.

'Oh hi Balish! Good afternoon ! Come, let's have lunch together today. Look, I've brought your favorite meatballs with stuffed cheese. Wanna have it'?

'No.... No.... Mr. Kahayan, I.... was just going for my own lunch. Mom has already packed a great amount of rice with boiled broccoli. I just hate it. I wish to eat your tasty meatballs, but'...

'Oh no problem boy. I'll help you in finishing your broccoli rice. I love it'.

Balish couldn't refuse him now. They ate food together. Christopher ate food alone, as he was angry with Balish.

That day, in the Supersonics class, the wizardry physics and in the English classes, Christopher wasn't present. He just sat desperately with Fredrick. Balish saw him and laughed.

'Oh hi Christopher my friend. Sitting with your new friend hmm? What's special in him that you're sitting with him'?

'Hey, I didn't ask you where to sit. Mind your own investigation business and I hope that you won't succeed in these things'.

Balish sighed and left the room. He took a quill and a parchment and sat near the fireplace where wizards could write letters anytime. He wrote,

Dear Christopher,

Sorry for my behavior. We were friends, did not we? So why are you angry? But yes, that case was a bit complicated. That's why I ignored you that time. Leave it now friend. Lets be friends again.

Your Friend,

Balish Lane

He used Iogy for delivering the letter, which was delivered in just a minute. Christopher read it and replied,

Dear Balish my friend,

I'm also sorry for my behavior. I annoyed you a lot but you didn't mind. Both of us were at fault. Let's be friends again. Will yah be?

Your friend,

Christopher Laurence

A domestic pigeon was passing by when Christopher held it by the neck and tied its letter quickly as the pigeon was hooting a lot and pinching Christopher on the face. It flew here and there. There wasn't any guarantee that he's going straight to Balish.

Christopher waited for Balish for coming and hugging him saying 'MY FRIEND'! But 2 days passed. Balish was seen nowhere. He stayed in his class only. Christopher thought correctly. The domestic pigeon had delivered the letter to Fredrick.

He read it and his eyebrows went upwards. He moaned.

'Oh my God ! a sorry letter to Balish? Whoa man! I can't believe it! But it'll be fun in teasing them. Yes'!

It was the 2nd of October. Mr. Hulhuge was announcing the first XI names for the league. The children, especially wizards were very excited.

'So... children and my dear wizards, are you ready for our squad? Listen, shout just after hearing ALL the names, he smiled.

The children shouted, 'Yes sir'!

'The first wizard and our captain is... Credpolio Root.'

Friends of Credpolio were clapping and the wizards were also happy. He was an experienced player too.

'Second we have Mora Leka'.

Balish felt pleased and Mora was very happy. His heart was lurching and dancing.

'Then we have -Smoplores Gredaria.

Xendra Neesham.

Tresaria Iodios.

Carlos Fander.

Danny Braithwaite.

Whurchiles Smeady.

Peter Moore',

Balish got tensed now. He prayed for his name.

'Fredrick Alwoy'...

'What!!! Fredrick'? The most inexperienced player in our team? It's ridiculous man, shouted the wizards.

'SILENCE IF YOU WANNA KNOW THE LAST NAME OF OUR SQUAD', said Mr. Hulhuge in a huge tone.

Fredrick fisted his hands and held it up.

'So wizards, our last member is... WARSLOW DAVICH'!

Balish was stunned as if someone had put a Stunning charm on him. He was standing as a statue while the others were jumping up and down. He wasn't inexperienced. At least he played better than Fredrick. But he wasn't in the starting XI.

'Don't be sad other wizards. The 4 substitutes are still left. Maybe your name may come this time'.

Balish didn't react. His dream was ALMOST broken.

'Our substitutes are-

Chickava Motovo;

Derlam Azario;

Polina Treshlink &

Balish Lane !

Mora cheered for Balish, who left a small smile now. He was happy, as he knew that he would obviously get a substitute for Fredrick or Tresaria, the topmost inexperienced players in their squad.

That day during lunch break, Fredrick came near to Balish and pushed him by the shoulders deliberately.

'Oh sorry! By the way, what happened to you? What did you say, that whatever I say would be same to me? But no! The case has taken a U-turn. And look at this. A sorry letter no? Do you love to trouble your friends? Oh at least you would have left your best friend, Christopher Laurence. You didn't take pity on him too. Hahaha'.

Balish ignored him and snatched the letter. Mr. Kahayan saw him.

'Hi Balish! You are a substitute, no? Happy feeling I'm having for you.

'Oh hi Mr. Kahayan. Not feeling happy for me? Hey I'm in the first XI! Say congrats to me', Fredrick said in the middle of talk to annoy Balish.

'Why congrats to you? And however, you are going to be substituted very soon in the match', Mr. Kahayan said so that Balish doesn't get angry.

'Rightly said Mr. Kahayan', Balish hi-fived Mr. Kahayan.

'WELCOME LADIES AND GENTLEMEN, WIZARDS AND KIDS! THIS IS THE MOST EXCITING LEAGUE OF THE HISTORY, WHICH IS GOING TO BE HELD AT THE NATIONAL QUIDDITCH STADIUM, SPONICZER, SONICLAND AND THE HOST OF THIS LEAGUE IS THE SUPERSONICS' INTERNATIONAL SCHOOL OF WIZ-WITCHCRAFTRY! I AM PLEASED TO GET A CHANCE TO ANCHOR THIS CHAMPIONSHIP. AND YES, OUR FIRST MATCH WILL BE PLAYED TODAY, BETWEEN THE SUPERSONICS' AND THE WALKRYS'!!!!!!! Said the anchor.

The wizards of the Supersonics' were cheered up, including the substitutes. The Walkrys' were snapping their fingers and smoothening their broomsticks, as the Supersonics' were nothing for them.

Coach Jimmy Leka was explaining some tricks to the wizards for defeating Walkrys'. On the other side, the opponents were drinking juices of different wizardry flavors.

Suddenly when Balish was wearing his Quidditch robes, a soft feathery hand patted him. It was Iogy. She was carrying a letter. Balish opened it, which read only 5 words,

ALL THE BEST,

SLIDDORY LAURENCE

It was the letter of his father. Balish kissed it and thought about his mother. He saw up and prayed for blessings. He thanked Iogy for the letter by giving her the Pigeon food.

In the stadium, the strikers- Captain Credpolio Root and Mora Leka were ready to kick-off the ball as per their coach. Balish was sitting on his broomstick and his hands were on his chin.

'SO ARE YOU READY? 3...2...1... PHHHHHHHHHH'!

The whistle blew. The strikers were off with the shining new ball on the stick. Suddenly when Credpolio was in the penalty corner, the opponent captain Jango Redseer tackled the ball and took it until the Supersonics' penalty corner. The defenders Fredrick and Tresaria were sweating in the chilly weather.

Jango slightly and very comfortably passed the ball through them saying, 'See yooou'. His English accent was very poor.

The goalkeeper, Werchiles Smeady also sweated and failed to stop the speedy ball whooshed by Jango Redseer.

'GOAL'! Said the Anchor.

The Walkrys' fans cheered, 'EASSSST OR WEZT, WALKRYS ARE THEEEE BEZT'!

Jimmy got angry. He quickly substituted Tresaria with Polina Treshlink. He was better than Tresaria. Fredrick frowned and went into the pavilion, faraway from Balish to avoid the teasing.

Again Mora and Credpolio were ready for the kickoff. The whistle blew again. Jango Redseer succeeded once more in tackling the ball from Mora.

In the pavilion, coach Jimmy Leka was banging his fists on the wall. Balish was tensed. The Walkrys' were proving to be heavy on their team.

'Coach, give me a chance please. Substitute me with Smoplores. I won't let you down', asked Balish very faithfully.

Mr. Jimmy couldn't understand what to do. Smoplores was really not doing anything in the form of a mid-fielder. He was just failing to tackle the ball from Jango and Rogan Locster, another fellow mate of Jango.

Finally he pressed the substitute button beside the coaches' seat. The anchor announced the substitute.

'So it is Balish Lane in, Smoplores Gredaria out'.

Balish had a great opportunity to show his skills. He wasn't an expert obviously, but better than Smoplores, who had sighed, the opposite of Fredrick when he returned back.

The match continued, and due to Balish's tackling, Supersonics' were almost near to the Walkrys' (9-12).

But the time was almost over. It was already 87 minutes out of 90. The Walkrys' took a timeout, which gave rest to Supersonics' too.

They made a circle in the pavilion. Jimmy Leka was telling some tricks.

'That wriggly pot shouldn't have chosen Werchiles as the goalkeeper. Now we don't even have a spare choice. Now we don't have to defend. We have to attack. Don't worry if the opponent reaches until the penalty corner. Everyone should not come. The defenders are there to defend. You attack and score as fast as you can. Credpolio, everything is on you now', explained him as he patted the captain on his back.

Probably the last whistle blew. The clash went on. Credpolio managed to tackle the ball with the help of Carlos Fander and Balish. In the penalty corner, Credpolio jumped the ball up and Carlos whooshed the ball straight into the goalpost.

'GOAL'! Shouted the anchor as the Supersonics' fans got up to their feet and they cheered. But luck wasn't with them for a long time. Very soon Jango and his mate Rogan made their way to 20th GOALS in no time.

The last 10 seconds were left. The score was 20-18. Credpolio made his way to the corner and he scored a goal. But the time was over just.

'OOOOOOH DEAR! WHAT A MATCH IT WAS! WHAT A TRY OF COMEBACKING BY THE SUPERSONICS TEAM! BUT UNFORTUNATELY, IT ISN'T THEIR DAY. THE WALKRYS' HAVE WON THE MATCH BY A GOAL' shouted the anchor as usual.

The team was dejected. They blamed each other for the loss. Where the Supersonics' lost to the Walkrys', on the other side the Yugados' lost to the Quiddos' by a large amount of goals (21 goals). So as per that, the Supersonics' were at the 3rd place with -1 points.

'Hssssh, at least not last', said Fredrick as if he has done something remarkable.

'Oh my god! Because of you, Fredrick, we have lost. If... If you would have just stopped that goal swooped by the opponent's captain... who was it... oh yes Jango Redseer, then we would have tied the match at least', said coach Mr. Jimmy angrily.

Fredrick smiled and went in the dressing room.

'Weezaardz, Wee haf wun our firsst mach verrry meeerely. Don't take dem laeeghtly at alll', said Jango Redseer to his team, from which only some understood his ruddy language. After that Jango explained it in his mother tongue.

'So wizards, our performance was not bad at all. No problems if we lost, but now we have to concentrate on our next match, which is probably against the Quiddos', said Mr. Hulhuge in a calm voice.

But the children were anxious. How could they fight against the strongest Quidditch team of their city?

'My boys, you'll have to accept this challenge at any cost. If we lose this match, then our chances of joining the semis will almost be over. Then we'll have to be depended on other teams'.

Soon it started raining. The assembly was cancelled

and it was the sonic-power period, which Mr. Jorge always took.

'Good morning students', said in a low tone. His throat wasn't fine that day.

The children greeted him.

'So, lost your first match of that boring sport.... Hmmm... what is it... Quidd...Quidditch... Ah yes! Quidditch. Why are you concentrating on these types of funny activities? Concentrate on studies. If you wanna be a successful person in life, then study as much as you can', Mr. Jorge said while clearing his throat.

The girls accepted this, as they weren't interested in Quidditch.

'But sir, all studies and no play makes us a dull person no'? Said curious Harold.

Mr. Jorge left a humph and took the chalk. He wrote many things, which the children desperately wrote. 5 periods passed & it was lunch. Mr. Kahayan approached and patted Mr. Jimmy on the shoulders.

'No problem coach. Better luck next time'.

Mr. Jimmy just smoothened his hair and said, 'Thanks Kahayan. Maybe your good words give a light of hope to my anxious wizards'.

Fredrick tiptoed and passed just beside Mr. Kahayan, who saw him and bent his eyebrows downwards and left a scary look.

Luck didn't give support to the Supersonics' in the next match too. They lost very badly (5-27). And because of that, they reeled to the 4th and to the last place.

'Oh this' wa' a left hand's work d' defeat' these puny inexperienced players', said Quiddos' captain Serdio Hundary in his rich British accent to his teammates. They had a party that day as they had qualified for the finals.

The next match was Supersonics' v/s the Yugados'. Yugados were on the 2nd place with +2 points. The Supersonics' were struggling by -23 points, and Jimmy Leka said, 'Our game is over boys. Now we can play only for pride'.

'No sir. If we win by more than 25 goals and a tiebreaker, then we can qualify', said Balish with a hope.

'Oh man! That's impossible! How can we score 26 goals more than the Yugados'? Tell me', said Fredrick, putting salt on the wounds.

'You're right Fredrick. How can we win when there's a player like you? Sir, I think we can take Polina Treshlink instead of Fredrick Alwoy. It will be better', said Mora.

Jimmy nodded and announced the starting XI to the anchor in a meeting.

'Uh um, so sir, we have 2 changes in our starting XI. Instead of Tresaria Iodios and Fredrick Alwoy, we're keeping Balish Lane and Polina Treshlink. I hope that by these changes, we may win by a great amount. However, our chances are almost over'.

'As you wish coach Mr. Jimmy Leka', said Mr. Neaten De Kock, boss of Ministry of Quidditch Meetings.

'THE TIME HAS COME FOR THE DECISION

GUYS! IT'S THE LAST LEAGUE STAGE MATCH, BETWEEN THE YUGADOS' AND THE SUPERSONICS'. IF SUPERSONICS' WIN BY MORE THAN 25 GOALS, THEN THEY CAN QUALIFY. BUT IF NOT, THEN SAY BYE-BYE TO THE FINALS' said the anchor, with a shining new mike.

It was the kickoff of the Yugados'. Their strikers, Forter Ogral and Martin Bloomsberg were ready for the whistle.

When the whistle blew, just as Ogral smashed the ball to the Supersonics' penalty corner, Mora jumped from his broomstick and dodged the ball. He covered a bit distance and passed it to Polina, who passed it to Peter and Warslow and finally to Credpolio, who was waiting in the Yugados' penalty corner. He just very easily tackled the ball by Yugados' defender Hredcig Kolino and straight in the goalpost.

'IT'S A GOAL IN THE VERY 1ST MINUTE GUYS'! Said the anchor.

They scored many historical goals and by the half time, the Yugados' were reeling 23-0 just due to the sheer great game, particularly of Balish Mora and the teammates hi-fived each other with a great snap.

Coach Jimmy Leka said,

'Just 2 more goals at least, and then maintain it. Beautiful playing guys! Keep it up'.

Mora and Balish's eyes had rage. They heard the whistle and started dodging the ball. They reached the corner when Ogral just pushed Balish and he fell down.

He got injured. His right wrist got a cramp. His right knee started bleeding. Obviously Ogral got a purple card, due to which Yugados' had only 10 players, and the Supersonics' got a penalty.

'Hey! Are you mad or what? Balish, get up. Can you? Asked Mora nervously.

'Ouch! I can't, Mora. Get me up fast please. Ouch', said Balish with a sweating face.

The therapists came and took Balish on their broomsticks.

Balish had to be re-substituted by Smoplores Gredaria. Mr. Jimmy made him mid-fielder.

Mora managed to get another goal in the penalty chance, due to which the score was now 24-0. The last 10 minutes were left. FINALLY, Martin Bloomsberg managed to score a single goal. The crowd was silent. Even if Yugados' defended 24 goals, then they would go to the finals. But no. In the last minute, Credpolio and Smoplores hit 1-1 goals respectively and the score was now 26-1.

'10...9...8...'

Mora speeded with his broomstick and passed the ball to Peter.

'7...6...5...'

He passed the ball quickly to Xendra, who was in the pen-corner. He dodged the ball until Mora came for support. Then he dodged and came in the D portion where the goalpost was only meters away.

'4.... 3...2...'

He threw the ball in the air.

'1....'

And he swooshed it into the goalpost.

'GOALLLLLLL! IT'S A GOAL AT THE VERY LAST SECOND! AND THE SUPERSONICS' WIN BY 26 GOALS, THAT MEANS THE SCORE IS 27-1! WHOA MAN! THE SUPERSONICS' HAVE QUALIFIED FOR THE FINAL, WHICH IS AGAINST THE QUIDDOS' INSTITUTE OF PRO QUIDDITCH LEARNING! THEY HAVE CREATED HISTORY! GREAT! ABSOLUTELY WONDERFUL'!

The crowd cheered. They were on their feet. Mr. Jimmy cried with joyful tears. Mora went to the dressing room, where Balish was lying down on the bed.

'I know what news you've brought. We have won, but not qualified. I'm right no'? Said Balish, with teardrops in his eyes.

'No Balish. Not only we won, but we have qualified for the finals too! The score is 27-1. Come sit on my stick. Let's celebrate'.

'WHAT! COME, LETS CELEBRATE'! Said Balish eagerly.

They celebrated their win with great excitement, especially Balish without caring about his wound.

'That's brilliant my boy! Keep it up! I'll surely watch you playing the final! Sorry I couldn't watch today's match, but I'm not gonna miss the final', said Mr. Laurence on Christopher's mini-top, unaware of Balish's cramp and wounds.

In the meeting of the discussion of the squads in the finals, Balish also attended. He wanted to know about his playing or not. However the final was on 26th October and the present date was 21th October.

'So Mr. Kurten, as the coach of the Quiddos', what's your squad', asked Mr. Neaten while clearing his throat.

'Sorry, but I doo naught know proper eenglish. But yess, my squad will bee same. No chenges at all', said Mr. Kurten, perturbed.

'O...Ok... as you wish sir, and Mr. Jimmy, any changes in your team or you also the same'?

Balish, with his eyes towards Mr. Jimmy, saw him with wide eyebrows. Jimmy also saw him and stammered.

'Umm... N...Yes...No...No...No changes sir. Our squad is also the SA...same', sweated Jimmy.

Balish breathed a sigh of relief as Mr. Kurten and the 2 coaches shook hands with each other.

'So...All the best coaches are beside me. See yah on the finals' eve.

They shuffled smiles and departed from the room, with Balish who was comfortable on his wand.

'Balish, I've selected you in the starting XI, but if you do anything wrong, then we can't do anything. You were the star of the match against the Yugados' by scoring 15 goals and gaining a penalty, and that's why we made it easier to score more than 25 goals against that team, but against the Quiddos', it'll be more difficult to even maintain a lead', said Mr. Jimmy with a sign of warning to Balish.

'Ah... don't worry coach. Everything will be fine. I'll not upset you'.

Two days later, in the chemistry lab, while finding a medicine for his cramp and wound, Fredrick saw him.

'Oh hi lovely boy. Feeling better or not? Oh no man, only 3 days to go! Will you be able to even sit on your magical wand? I'm very much worried for you'.

'You don't care about our school's reputation, so why are you saying about me? 10 players except me are still there, and 4...oh sorry I mean 3 substitutes are there to handle the matter. So you SHUT your mouth', replied Balish.

Fredrick didn't say anything after that. He just left the lab, while Balish noticed Mr. Hulhuge in the corridor.

'Sir...Sir... a minute please'...

'Oh hi my boy... my star... Balish... careful', said cheerful Hulhuge.

'Sir, I've heard that you know about medicines a lot, so can you please help me to find the cure of my wound... I'm in the starting XI'.

'I'm not sure about the right medicine for your wounds exactly, but yes, a special wizard medicine comes named Desprocyl. It's cheap ... around 3 Euros only. All the best... I wanna see at least 10 goals... Hahaha'!

'Thanks sir. And yes... I'll try to score.

That day, Balish had to open his truth in front of Mr. Laurence if he wanted to buy the particular medicine.

'Oh my! What the...! Who did it? How did he do it... When did he do it... tell me Balish... How'll you play in the final match'!

'Dad, while playing Quidditch against the Yugados', their defender pushed me off the wand and I fell down. Now no argument please... I'm in the starting XI and I'm gonna play for my team'.

Sliddory wanted to argue, but Balish wasn't in a mood at all. Christopher patted him and along with Mrs. Laurence and they went to buy the medicine (Desprocyl).

That medicine proved useful, and in 3 days, Balish was fit enough to play.

'SO LADIES AND GENTLEMEN... WIZARDS AND WITCHES... ARE YAH READY'?

'YES'! Was the word from the enchanting crowd.

'AS WE ALL KNOW... TODAY IS THE FINAL OF THE INTER-SCHOOL QUIDDITCH LEAGUE 2016-17, BETWEEN THE SUPERSONICS' INTERNATIONAL SCHOOL OF WIZ-WITCHCRAFTRY AND...THE QUIDDOS' SCHOOL OF PRO QUIDDITCH LEAGUING'...

'YEAH! WHOOOOO! QUI...DDOS... QUID...DOS...'

'LADIES & GENTLEMEN, please maintain silence...

The crowd became silent.

'THAT'S BETTER... FIRST OF ALL WE WOULD LIVELY SEE THE TOSS BETWEEN THE TWO CAPTAINS, CREDPOLIO ROOT AND JANGO REDSEER'!!!!!

'JANGO JANGO'!

Credpolio won the toss, and as per coach Jimmy's advice, he chose the kickoff.

'SO ALL PRESENT HERE... ARE YOU READY...'

The board in front of the stadium blinked. It showed many international Quidditch players counting backwards.

Balish saw them and excitedly shouted, 'Whoa!

'OH YES! I FORGOT TO SAY THAT TODAY WE GONNA HAVE A DINNER WITH THE RECENT QUIDDITCH WORLD CUP WINNERS, AUSTRALIAAAAA'!!!

The crowd and the players lost control now. They happily shouted as they could, ignoring the anchor when the wizard police agencies came and handled the matter.

'10 9 8 7 6 5 4... PLAY...IT...ONNNNNNNN'!

The whistle blew. Mora and Credpolio were on their way. They tackled the ball hit by captain Serdio Hundary which reached the penalty corner. But the defender saved it from Balish, who was fit and fine enough for this match.

'OOOH THAT WAS CLOSE'! everybody whispered!

He passed the ball far away to the striker Tim Serjio. He dodged the ball and reached the penalty corner, where Polina and Warslow were ready to safeguard Werchiles Smeady.

But Serdio Hundary was on his way. He reached the D and tackled the ball easily from Polina Treshlink. He whistled and flickered the ball into the goalpost, opposite side of Werchiles.

'IT'S A GOAL! ....ITS 1-0'!

Balish bent on his wand with heads down. Fredrick was begging for a substitute from Jimmy, who had to accept and pressed the substitute button.

'SO ITS FREDRICK ALWOY IN, POLINA TRESHLINK OUT'.

He happily went into the penalty corner beside Warslow. Fredrick hi-fived him, who ignored it.

Tim managed to score another goal. After half time, the score was 12-10.

'THE SITUATION IS VERY TIGHT! THE SUPERSONICS' ARE MASTERS IN COMEBACKING, SO THE NEXT HALF-TIME WILL BE PACKED WITH ACTION'...

In the next half time, Mora managed to score 3 goals, whereas Balish scored 2. The score after 88 minutes was 20-19. The Quiddos' took a strategic timeout.

'We're in the lead coach! Just 2 more minutes and the trophy is ours', said Balish eagerly.

'Yes my boy! And you... Fredrick... you stay in the midfield and Mora, you please stay in the penalty corner for defending a goal and chances for the trophy'.

The whistle blew once more and probably the last time.

Something unfortunate was written for them. Serdio Hundary tackled the ball easily and obviously from Fredrick and Balish, where Mora hit his broomstick mistakenly, but costly.

'OOOOH IT'S A PENALTY IT'S A PENALTY'!!!!!!!!!!!!

Tim Serjio winked at Mora, who was red with anger. The Quidditch stadium was filled with clouds. It was a rainy weather. The anchor gave the penalty whistle fast so that the important task is completed.

Tim hit the goal under Werchiles' shoulder, though it touched him.

'ITS 20-20, AND ITS STARTED DRIZZLING GUYS! OH NO, THE WIND IS SPEEDING AND I THINK THIS MIXTURE IS GONNA COMPLETE INTO A TORNADO. I REQUEST ALL THE PARTICIPANTS TO RUSH TO THEIR RESPECTIVE ROOMS AND YES, WE'VE DECIDED THAT THE MATCH HAS TIED!!! THE PRESENTATION WILL BE POSTPONED FOR TOMORROW BUT THE DINNER WILL NOT BE... HAVE A GREAT DAY'!!!!!!

The crowd murmured to themselves and threw empty disposable glasses full of juices and sodas on the anchor ruthlessly, when the wizard police agencies somehow put metal parchments in front of the stadium, where the glasses put an impact a bit, but it didn't break.

'Are you serious? How can the match be tied? Means all our hard work has gone in vain'? Asked Werchiles.

'I'm really confused too, and I'll try to talk to the manager. You don't worry. Our school will get the trophy', said Mr. Jimmy anxiously.

They, not being worried about the finals' results, got overexcited for the dinner with the defending champs Australia.

'Dear kids, don't misbehave at all there. Yes, you can take autographs, but stay on your wands while having your dinner. We'll upload the photos in the annual wizardry magazine, where every year we used to publish the inter-House Quidditch League's photos, this year we're going to publish a lavish, trendy portfolio of the inter-school league', said Mr. Jorge, who had got a severe fever of the sport that he once said 'boring'.

It was almost 7. The agencies were steady with their stylish guns with a stamp on a red ribbon on each of them.

'Wow man! What a job we've got! We can meet any famous player anytime in an eye's blink', said an officer.

His fellow grinned instead of replying. Just then they heard the clicks of many cameras. The car had arrived. On the car's seat, headmaster Mr. Hulhuge was handling his tie and coat's collar.

The trumpets blew. The Aussies' got off. First of all Iron Layshout, the captain, shook his hand in the air while his fans came out of their nearby houses and crowded him.

The crowd increased and became so big that the agencies had to scare them away by shooting teargas bullets in the air.

There was mayhem. People ran back to their homes. Some ran and pushed people so fast that Iron wriggled and almost fell by a push when Mr. Hulhuge held him by the hand and pulled him back on his feet.

They stepped in the hall, where the wizards were waiting silently, and just as they saw the team, they got on their wands and rushed with their quills and parchments.

'One by one wizards! Don't misbehave'...

Fredrick Alwoy put his finger on his lips and they made a queue. No one paid attention on any other player than Iron.

There were a great variety of dishes. There was everything, from rice with stuffed meatballs, to bacon bling and golden sushi rolls. Their mouths automatically watered and saliva was falling as if they've drunk water and not swallowed it.

They had a fantastic dinner. Balish and Mora were returning home with the certificates.

'Great match and a great dinner. Well don't worry, my father... I mean coach Mr. Jimmy will see the matter', said Mora while they parted ways towards their homes.

Mr. and Mrs. Laurence were waiting for their child-champ. Iogy was sitting on Dad Sliddory's shoulder as it would be her perch. Christopher was sitting on the table and he wasn't amused. He was just sighing and waiting for his dinner.

'Welcome my boy! No problems if we didn't get the trophy, we are 1st too. See the news Balish'! Said Mrs. Laurence.

In the news, the reporters were telecasting the Quidditch final.

'So as you can see, the Inter-School Quidditch League ended in a tie, but... as in the first-half the Quiddos' were ahead by 2 points, and in the 2nd half, the Supersonics' scored 2 extra points, so looking all the statistics and as per LSD (Later-on scoring decisions), the winners are the Supersonics'!

'Whoa! It's great! That means that the trophy will be presented to us in tomorrow's presentation! I can't wait for the moment when we'll be famous worldwide', shouted Balish with a tight glimpse on the television.

Where the winners were enjoying and celebrating their sudden win, there was anger in the camp of the Quiddos'.

'How can they do this with us? I can totally, without any doubt say, that they have done match fixing', said captain Serdio Hundary with his visible head and neck nerves.

Credpolio, the very next day before the presentation, hugged Balish and said.

'Oh, did you watch the news yesterday? We have won! I'm really happy. If we've won, we've won because of you versus the Yugados', if you wouldn't have scored the precious goals, then we couldn't even enter the finals'.

Balish cleared his throat and winked back while he went near the opponent captain, Serdio Hundary.

'Congrats bro. You had won against us in the league stage. And thanks too, because you defeated Yugados' by a large amount and made our way clear'.

'Oh... yes... hmm... con... congrats... to... you too... hehehe'...

He ran behind the stage with a red face.

'Welcome viewers as we all know that today is a special presentation of the final guys. As all happened, yesterday night we had a meeting of the coaches. After a prolonged discussion, we decided that as per the LSD, the Supersonics' are the winners'!

Almost all the viewers were excitedly watching their children (wizards) that they'll get the trophy. The Quiddos' had not subscribed the MoonQuidditch channel deliberately after listening the news.

'First of all, we have the most energized player of the league from... the Walkrys' and the player is... obviously captain Jango Redseer! No problem if they came 3rd... they have played for pride, and for distributing the medal; I'm calling Mr. Wyter the headmaster of the Walkrys'.

The group of people clapped as Jango waved his hand.

When the host asked his experience, then Jango said,

'Wee laust so whaat... At leest wee gaut a chance to pley and notheeng is better. I am vary gratfuul to Mr. Hulhuge, the hedmastar of the Supersonics' that thaey choz our skool'.

'Hmmm... a great experience! Thanks... now it's time to present the player who scored the most goals, and I know that you are aware who is it... its Balish Lane of the Supersonics'!

'Are yah serious? Me... I've scored the most numbers of goals'? Said Balish to himself.

He hesitated a bit, and finally waved his hands and got the medal, which Mr. Wyter was giving with a pat on the back and an unlikely smile. Balish couldn't understand that expression, and he scuttled towards the host.

Mr. and Mrs. Laurence were clapping and tears of joy were dropping off their chins. Iogy also cooed. Christopher was surprised. He didn't watch the match of Supersonics' v/s Yugados', so he was not so excited.

'So... Balish what was your experience in this packed, fun-filled league? I know you must be happy that your school did a great comeback and won the final due to the LSD system'.

'Yes Sir, I was very excited before the league, and if I want to give the credit to anyone, then he is my brother, Christopher Laurence, my parents, Mr. and Mrs. Laurence and my great headmaster, Mr. Hulhuge Morgan'...

Christopher's ears and face shifted from the mini-laptop to the television, where his kind brother was giving credit to him.

'Oh look Christopher; he's giving credit to you too. At least now spit your anger', said Mrs. Laurence, whose eyes were overloaded with joyful tears.

'You know mom these tears are wasteful. This credit like funny thing is a lie. He's just saying this to coax me. You just turn off this television, or else watch some other comedy programs. However, the number of these programs are so much', said Christopher, trying to discourage them.

'Aw, how can you be so rude Christopher? Learn something from Balish'! Said Mrs. Laurence.

Christopher murmured something to himself as he got up from the table, taking Iogy's perch with him, where Iogy was flattering his wings and hooting, as she wanted to see the live telecast when Mr. Laurence snatched the perch and left a grin.

'Great my boy. You can come with your friends. Viewers it's time for a break and after that, we'll have the champions Supersonics' in the trophy ceremony and the most exciting ceremony of the final... the new wands distribution... Yes in this ceremony we now distribute new wands with a rich golden color'!!!

Alfred watching this all. He thought to write a letter to Balish. He wrote-

Dear Balish,

Congratulations on your great, stunning win in the Quidditch Inter-School League. You're the most goal-scoring player no? I send you warm regards. Keep it up.

Your Friend,

Alfred Jones

But he was in a problem. There wasn't any pigeon in their home, so he had to find a domestic pigeon nearby to deliver the letter. Luckily, a pigeon was flying by when Alfred caught him. He tied the letter and the pigeon flew away.

* * *

- CHAPTER -

8

Christopher's Bet

At the Laurence' home, the parents were trying to inveigle Christopher as he was irritated by the win of Balish's team.

'What's this nonsense? Balish is about to return home with a shining medal and trophy, and it's truth with no doubt, that he's gonna give this trophy in your hands and here you are doing this fussy little drama', said Mr. Laurence angrily.

'Dad, I think you are creating a fuss of a nonsense. What happened if Balish's team has won any inter-school competition? If he has the guts, then tell him to compete with the international players and yes, when he wins, I'll accept that he's really a champ'.

'Ok... Ok then... I assure that he'll play at the international level, but not Quidditch. Any other sport you choose, and you see, when Balish achieves incredible heights, then you'll not even reckon to tease him', said Mr. Laurence with a shine of hope.

Balish returned home with the trophy as he pressed the bell. Mrs. Laurence opened the door and hugged him so tightly that Balish couldn't breathe.

'Mom, I'm struggling! Leave me fast'.

'My child, I was waiting for you only. You've proved yourself today by your courage and excellent performance. Come inside, your father is waiting for you, said Mrs. Laurence.

'Before dad, I wanna meet Christopher. Where's he? I thought that he'll welcome me and hold the trophy glancing it, but he's not even visible'.

'Don't worry Balish. Maybe he's in his room. You can meet him, but first sit for a moment'.

'I'll sit in my room and discuss the strange problem that why my brother didn't welcome me', said Balish angrily as he went towards his room.

The argument between Mr. Laurence and Christopher was over. Mr. Laurence was in his room while Christopher was busy in his mini-laptop. Just then Balish knocked the door as if any V.I.P. was sitting inside.

'Can I come in, Mr. Christopher Laurence', said Balish deliberately.

Christopher was surprised by the behavior of Balish. He said, 'Come in'.

Balish opened the door and closed it. He still thought that Christopher will hug him and praise him for the recognition he got in the presentation, but Christopher was playing a game and when he lost, he groaned and threw a pillow on Balish.

'All because of you. I was so close to my hi-score, and you came and put your poor sights on my game', said Christopher shamelessly.

'Oh really', said Balish as he was ready to discuss in a proper manner and he kept his trophy on the table, 'all because of ME? I mentioned your name happily that that win is because of you, and you aren't even welcoming me despite watching the telecast'?

'Yes so what? Did I say to mention my name? Did I say to blame me for the win'? Said Christopher with a high tone.

Balish was heartbroken. He didn't expect this type of behavior from Christopher at all. He made his way out of the room, towards Dad Sliddory's room. There he came to know about the matter.

'And you said yes! How can I win any international game at the age of 12'? Said Balish, sweating.

'I... I can't change my decision my boy... but yes. I've said specifically that you can play in international level at any sport you like... and I'll choose one of the perfect coaches...'

'Dad, no coaches only home training. It's the perfect mantra for a perfect performance', interrupted Christopher.

'We didn't ask you anything, but if you're saying... then... ok... no... no coaches for the sake of Balish's ability', said Mr. Laurence.

Balish's eyes widened as if he saw or heard any macabre thing. His body had split from the inner part. Training without a coach was understandable, but at the international level was impossible. But he had to accept this challenge.

'I'm ready Christopher. For your faith, I'll do anything', said Balish.

'That's expectable my brother', moaned Christopher.

The next day, Balish uncomfortably went to school. He sat alone, as his partner Harold Milky was absent. The very first period was physics (Mr. Jorge was in a good mood that day).

He whistled and came inside the class, patting Fredrick Alwoy who was late that day too, as usual.

'Go to your seat, don't be late next time'.

'Th...Thanks sir. I promise I'll be early tomorrow', said Fredrick, whose eyes ignored tensed Balish.

'So children, today we'll learn how to make spells. It's a very easy formula, and it can be used for many purposes. For example- the reddish color chemical, which is called clodorole2, helps in washing your clothes anti-detergent, the yellowish-green color one is called swiftofy. It's a unique type of spell. It helps in learning some sports, like classic chess and leisure hockey too'...

Aha! That was the mantra that Balish could use to learn any sport. He would be thankful to God that Christopher wasn't in the class that time. He had gone to the toilet.

'Sir, I have a question. Can I please talk to you after the class personally? I have a serious problem', said Balish, who had almost got the solution to the bet.

'Of course my champ you meet me in the staff room. I'll discuss your problem, said Mr. Jorge cheerfully.

After the class was over, Balish went along with anxious and curious Jorge. Christopher suspiciously saw them and tried to follow them, but normal children weren't allowed in the staff room.

After the discussion was over, Mr. Jorge left a sigh.

'Oh my god this is such a puny problem and you're saying it serious? I'll give you 2 cauldrons full of this spell, but you don't be tensed'.

Really, there was a thick layer of yellowish-green liquid, which was squirting out of the cauldron in drops.

Balish handled it carefully, poured the liquid in his elixir bottle, which he had already drunk before lunch and when half a cauldron was left, he borrowed a bottle from Sir Jorge.

'Thank you sir I'll return this bottle as fast as I can. Am... Yes there are no side effects of this spell no... I suppose', said Balish nervously.

'I think yes there is a side effect. If you over-use this spell I mean drop this spell non-purposely then you will shrink in size and maybe if you spill it mistakenly, then your life can also be at cost, so be careful', said Mr. Jorge as Balish hid the bottles behind his robes.

Christopher forgot to ask Balish the reason of entering the staff room, which was good for him.

That day at home, Balish quickly ate his food; ignoring the television Christopher had opened to castigate him. He perched Iogy on his shoulders and went up in his room's toilet.

He remembered the effects of the spell, so he warned Iogy especially by his wand.

'Hmmm, so that's how to use this spell. Iogy, can you fetch me a bottle of Yakult from the nearby generator'? Said Balish confidently.

Iogy cooed and flew from the washroom's window, which was like an entrance for Iogy.

She returned with a whoosh in no time, with a bottle full of Yakult held on her talons.

'Great'! Said Balish.

He drank the Yakult and emptied the bottle. After that he poured the chemical in the bottle, which filled in no time. Next he gave the ready spell to Iogy and she dropped it straight on the head of Balish.

Crack!

The bottle cracked and the spell started doing its effect. Balish's mind and hands-legs started shaking. He automatically jumped up and down with his hands reaction changing on jump.

Iogy was panicked. She cooed and tried to stop Balish, who refused and told the reason of his ups and downs.

After 10 minutes, the effect disappeared. Balish sighed and was happy that his scratch didn't hurt him during the procedure.

He called Christopher and Mr. Laurence for testing the spell.

'Now what new drama are you going to create? Don't you know we've got a project to do in the weekends'? Said Christopher irritably.

Balish got annoyed and ignored him and instead challenged him for a sport. Christopher chose chess and it was confirmed that the winner is going to be Balish.

The board appeared by a tap of his wand on the table. Christopher wasn't surprised and he chose white.

He drove his horse unwisely, blinking at Balish.

Balish took the chance and drove his pawn above the queen. His mind was shaking and Balish had an experience that the mind is telling the trick.

After 2 minutes, Christopher was checkmated and he was sweating.

'What's up bro? Got satisfaction or not yet'? Said Balish with a wink to Christopher.

'Hey, you said international! But this isn't international'!

'So what? I thought you were the champ of chess in classes'.

'I specially told dad that you'd play at International level, that too without a coach'.

'Stop your argument boys! I know that he has to play at a particular level, but he was just testing your ability, and this match shows that Balish is better than you, Christopher Laurence'! Said Mr. Laurence very angrily and crankily.

Christopher's face went pale, then red.

'So if that's the matter, then I bet you, before this semester ends, you have to find out the mystery about the construction going on in the forest, and I will take a photo of the Inferno Lord, then only I would accept you as my brother.'

Balish also fell pale. He couldn't believe what his brother had said right now. Just then Mrs. Laurence, thank god unaware of the recent bet called them for dinner.

It wasn't a good dinner that day. Christopher had lost his own television remote; Balish had forgot to bring Iogy's food because of the argument and Mrs. Laurence forgot to buy vegetables for the routine salad due to a regular medical check-up of hers.

'Oh my god! What did I think and what happened'! Said Mrs. Laurence.

'What did you think honey'? Asked Mr. Laurence curiously.

'I thought we'll have a great meal of French Meatballs-Rice with rich tomato chutney, but because of the mayhem... I mean regular checkup, I forgot everything'.

The trio (Mr. Laurence, Balish and Iogy) sighed. Christopher was eating his food grumpily as he was missing his favorite television show. He finished his food and went in his room with the intention of finishing his project of writing all the properties of dark creatures, which were available only in a tiny village in South Vatican City.

Due to the small place and deserted location, the mini-laptop was also unable to find out the location and Christopher refused to ask help from Balish certainly.

Balish whistled and entered the room, as he knew how to finish the task (he would use his wand as a broom and go to Vatican City by using the instant reaching spell.

He did it. He went to Vatican City in the dead of the night, when dogs were barking strangely. But when he reached there, he saw something very unusual. The homes were made up of zippers, and the front doors were zipped up. Balish took some photos in his mini-top and moved ahead.

Suddenly the detector blinked and made directions. Balish ran towards those directions and he found the village. There, a man was standing with a torch in his hand on the other side. Balish saw him and asked him, stammering,

'Wh...Who are you... and wha...what are you doing here'?

'Oh hi friend... I knew it that you'll come...'

'MORA'!

'BALISH'!

They were face to face. They laughed and hugged each other.

'Whoa man you and here'! Said Mora.

'Now it isn't the time to be curious. Let's proceed and do our project'.

'Wait a minute. Werchiles Smeady is also here somewhere. We came together and we parted ways to find the location...

Werchiles can join us'.

He came from behind and wished Balish.

They found out the location, gossiping about the bet.

'Ok... So that's the matter. Hmm... It's a bit funny but it can be dangerous if Christopher becomes serious', said Werchiles.

They reached the village and started investigation.

'Be careful, I've only heard that if they meet predators, then they can bite us off too', whispered Mora.

'Don't scare us Mora PLEASE'! Said Werchiles.

Balish nodded his head and sighed to himself. Just then a black beetle-type creature came in front of the trio, screeching.

'See what's in front of us! It's a dark creature! It's what we wanted', sang Werchiles Smeady.

'Capture it in our cage we brought Werchiles AS... FAST... AS... YOU... CAAAAAAN'!!!! Said Mora.

'Oh yes... Kaboom '!

The creature was in the cage. It changed its color from blackish-grey to red, then generated some electricity and broke the cage in a second. Then it ran away, screeching again.

'This was expected my friends', said Balish without any surprise.

Werchiles' body turned stiff. Mora's mouth also opened wide.

'But yes... I have taken a photo of that black beetle-type thing. We can write the properties from that only and show 'em to Professor Ledger', said Balish, winking to the duo.

'You're great man! You are truly fantastic! We can print the photo too; that will be the evidence that we visited Vatican City and saw this creature', said Mora.

The next Monday, when Professor Ledger asked for the project, the trio showed the photo. Ledger didn't want any evidence, instead he needed the properties that they forgot to write and because of that, Ledger gave them poor marks (11 out of 20).

'No problems guys, we got at least +10 marks. Leave this Ledger Professor', said Balish, without any boo.

The next day was a special day. It was Christopher's birthday, and even he didn't know about it due to the irritation he created himself.

When he got up, Balish shouted and left a 'spunky' voice (he opened the snowy party can), and a gift was ready on Christopher's blanket.

'**Surprise**eee'!

'What... hey it's my...' he lowered his voice.

'Many many happy returns of the day my brother', said Balish.

Christopher, instead of hugging and thanking him, ignored him and went in the washroom to wash his face. Later he went downstairs for breakfast, where his favorite food, Baked Brinjal vegetable with rice and French Fries was organized by Balish.

'MOM, THIS ALL IS FOR ME BUT WHAT WAS THE NEED TO DO THIS', Shouted Christopher with laughter and excitement.

But to his surprise, Mr. and Mrs. Laurence were coming out of their room, yawning and opening eyes.

'Happy birthday my boy, may God bless all the happiness to you...' said Mrs. Laurence, then she saw all the food and got dumbfounded... 'Who brought this food and from where? Christopher, have you brought all this food from a 5 star hotel using your pocket money'?

'What? This isn't your deed, then who has done it'?

'Er... I tapped my wand on the table and the food appeared on my call. Actually I knew its Christopher's birthday and I already, with Iogy's help bought this food using my wand's power. Christopher, you can accept it as a 2nd gift from me', said Balish from the staircase.

'Wow, you care so much about Christopher, I didn't know', said Mrs. Laurence.

Christopher grinned and ate the food, thanking Balish in a faint, rough voice.

'Thanks' was the call.

Balish, after returning from school, sent Christopher to play anyhow and called Alfred and Mora for helping them decorate the house for a party.

'Great idea, I'll bring colorful balloons "Lucio", and by the chant, balloons fell from the ceiling and automatically hanged on the walls.

Alfred called many friends of theirs, including Harold and Polina Treshlink, who were playing with Christopher at that moment.

Until 7, the home was decorated. The invited guests were also on their way, which just passed by Christopher and the duo.

'Hey, hi friends, ready to go? Wait for us... Christopher, Polina and me have to change as we're going for a... no we're going somewhere outside with these boys and yes... again a happy birthday to you, said Harold who was just about to open the secret.

They mixed up with the boys and reached home as fast as they could. They wore their designer pants and shirts and in 5 minutes, they were ready to ring the bell of Christopher's home.

'Trinnnng'.

Balish opened the door and welcomed them inside.

'Yes yes, you've come just at the correct time. Christopher also must be on his way back to home'.

'Hey Balish... I think... we should hide in his room... at particular places and- and when he enters, we'll give him a... sur...prissssse', said Alfred who was taking long breathes and clamming with sweat.

'You take a calm breathe, and however your idea is excellent. We'll do as you are saying. Be ready guys, Christopher has come', whispered Harold.

Christopher entered and let out a shriek when he saw the decorations. Mr. and Mrs. Laurence were dressed in their fanciest dresses with a gift box in their hands. They hugged him and said.

'This all is also done by Balish and Alfred. Ok, first you dress up in your room, I've arranged it properly on your bed, and yes... don't say anything right now'.

Christopher tried to speak and deliberately annoy Balish, but he heard chuckles from the room and he almost understood the matter.

He tiptoed towards his room, where on the door side Mora was hiding and whispering something to others. He knocked the door, by which the children became alert immediately.

'Anyone there inside? Voices are coming, its too late now to be vigilant', said Christopher.

They all rushed under the bed, where Balish was squeezed like a lemon and about to scream for breath.

Christopher opened the door and saw the underside of the bed. The cloth that they used to hide themselves was moving due to the suffocation occurring there. Many whispery 'Ouches' could also be heard.

They couldn't stay longer. They came out leaving a loud and lengthy 'Surrrprisssse'!

'Oh you all and here? What's this all? Balish, enough is enough! I told you that there is no benefit of doing this all. I was angry, am angry, and will remain angry ok, so you all friends can return home without any hesitation. And yes, if you're hungry, ask food from Mora and Balish Lane. They'll help you by using their wands'.

'Enough is enough! I have done so much for you and you are not even showing pity on me? I thought as a brother you'll thank me, welcome me or at least wish me hello or hi, but if you're remaining in your obstinacy, then ok.

They all were dejected and went home with frowns and heads down. Mrs. Laurence, who was excited to host some fun games, was also wonderstruck. She asked the matter, but they all just made their route towards their homes.

'What's this Christopher? I thought that...'

'You think everything mom. I have warned Balish many times that he should not help me, but he is madly servicing me as if I'm his boss or anything. So please tell him, that if... if he does this type of thing, then there's no space for him in my room, and if he can't stay in the verandah or in the main room, then Alfred or Mora's home is also there, suitable for him', said Christopher, crossing the limits.

Balish said nothing to say after the long argument. Whatever Christopher said hurt him a lot. He just started packing his bags and in 10 minutes, he was ready to depart.

'Where are you going Balish? You can't do this! Stay in our home and don't take seriously whatever you brother has said as this is nothing but childish talks. If you leave, we cannot live without you, Said Mrs. Laurence.

'My sweet aunt, you have taken good care of me for a year and for all the services you provided, I'm grateful to you. Now, the time has come for me to go. Somewhere faraway from here, and I promise that I'll send letters to you, I will be in touch. You don't worry at all', and saying this, he took a photo of his and

Christopher and ignoring Mr. Laurence, he went out of the house, 'And yes Christopher, I hope you succeed in your bet you told'.

Mrs. Laurence started squalling. Christopher grinned and went out of his room, whistling instead of consoling his mother.

Balish was holding his bag over his shoulder and he just passed by Alfred 's house, where Alfred was not at home.

'What? Alfred is not here, then where is he'? Said Balish to Mrs. Jones, who was sobbing.

He became more upset. He now took his wand and started flying. He covered a long distance and reached an odd place where houses were there, but no people. There was a board, on which some notes were written in rich red ink.

This place has been banned for impure people. Impure in the sense that only people who are pure blood can live here. However, as the population is just like nothing, this village has been ransacked and only reptiles can enter due to the 'Leistacio' spell.

Balish had the wish to live here now alone. He knew that the freezing charm could stop him, but if 2 freezing charms intercepted, then the effect could be less from 2 days to 2 minutes, and then the spell would be blocked. Balish thought it is right to suffer 2 minutes being frozen, so he entered the village with a shout.

'Leistacio'!

When the spells intercepted, a jet of turquoise

color appeared and Balish froze. Crows cawed and sat on him.

After 2 minutes, the effect disappeared and Balish's paralyzed body became normal. He went inside the village and accidentally too deep. Then he noticed a house less cracked than the others. The reddish color of the bricks was visible. On the main board, something was scribbled. It was something written 'Mr. Lane.

Balish did not see that board and left a 'however-let's-enter' expression and opened the door and just as he opened it, something horrible was there.

A man was frozen and cockroaches and many insects were on it. Balish shouted 'KOLIAS' and all of the insects ran away due to the smell emitted from the charm left by Balish. It was the stale-smell charm, due to which any insect or animal would run away.

After a few minutes, the man was ok, though coughing.

'Hello sir. Can you hear me'? Said Balish.

He rubbed his eyes and tried to see him, and even tried to speak, because his throat was sore.

Though he could see Balish very faintly, he saw him and he saw an image of an infant inside Balish. **After all, he was his father.**

* * *

- CHAPTER -

9

The Cavity of Clandestine

Am I dreaming or what? Said Mr. Lane with flam in his throat.

Balish too, with a bizarre reaction, had a glance on his unrecognizable father and scratched his head.

'Sorry, but I think that you are lost in this village', said Balish.

Mr. Lane, with some struggle got up and stroked at his main door board, when he realized that it is his home, which had a lot of cracks.

'Did an upheaval come here...Ouch (it was hurting his head), what had happened due to which I'm stinking', said Mr. Lane, this time giving a 'ho-hum' which cleared his throat.

'Well, I think that you are correct, but if you see carefully, on the timber of your village, it is written that only pure blood is allowed here now. Due to the lack of population, this village has been weathered and a wall of a fully upgraded freezing charm has been put by the main lawmakers of this village', said Balish.

Mr. Lane had a stroke of fear and his heart missed a beat or two, when he heard the whistling wind and the sounds of crickets.

'So that means that I'm alone here'... Asked Mr. Lane with wide open eyes.

Balish nodded.

'Anyways, I have come here to ask you that can... can I live here with you and treat you as a father', said Balish.

'My boy, you can happily live here. It will be a great pleasure for me that someone is here to take care of me... well by the way if there was a wall of a freezing charm, then how did you enter', asked Mr. Lane curiously. Balish hesitated for a moment, and then finally told his truth.

'And why have you come here to live in this ill-healthy-looking village', asked Mr. Lane doubtfully this time.

'Actually, my mother had died, and one of the members of the family who adopted me, doesn't love me. So I thought to leave their home and stay somewhere else, and please don't force me to return to my home as I don't want to go. But if you don't want me to stay here, I can go from here right now, said Balish, this time non-hesitatingly.

'Oh why are you so angry? Of course you can live here, but I'm scared that I can't provide the facilities you had in your old home', said Mr. Lane, who was feeling better and leaving a sigh of relief.

Just in the middle of their chitchats, a whooshing sound of a broomstick was heard. Balish put his index finger over Mr. Lane mouth and told him to be silent using his hand.

The resonance became silent and it turned into the sound of boots. The man who was approaching, his breathings were also be able to be felt. His shadow was visible to the duo. Balish gulped and the man said in a recognizable voice, 'Balish'!

'W...Wait a minute... I have listened you somewhere... Er... Oh my... ALFRED', Balish said astoundingly.

They hugged each other and let the tears of great feeling and joy come out.

Mr. Lane scratched his head and interrupted with a ho-hum,

'Are you friends', guys'?

'Friend? He is like a brother to me. He's always with me in every good and bad situations, and you know, he even saved my mini-top from my tetchy brother, am I right Alfred', said Balish, still hugging Alfred.

'O...Ok then, now what we have to do is that first of all we have to bring water and at least a bit of food for our survival... I mean generally my survival, as I'm not a wizard', said Mr. Lane.

Balish laughed and took out his wand, which expanded in a useful tool.

'I'm off in search of food and water and the same will be easily available in close proximity. Alfred, you take care of our host', said Balish while he whooshed away. He had fetched a full pouch of water, and while he was searching for food by his set of magic binoculars, he saw Christopher, who was playing Quidditch with Mora and another lad.

'I think Mora is not aware of my absence, that's why he is chilled, otherwise'...Balish thought.

The ball which was accidentally stroked by Christopher in the air above the limited level was coming nearer and nearer to Balish, who was almost invisible to the duo from such a distance.

Mora shouted 'Leistacio'! And what happened was astonishing. Balish, as he was in the range of the ball, also got ice-covered. Mora took a minute to reach nearer the ball and he saw Balish.

'Oops, I think I've frozen your brother too. Sorry', he said to Christopher, who got stunned when he looked Balish in his protectorate.

'O...Oh yes. I noticed him play...playing with Werchiles and a few more friends and maybe... he might have been a hunt of... of your hex... hehehe', said Christopher assertively, though edgy.

Mora used his spell once more to make it intercept and Balish became normal. 'Where am I, and Mora, how did you come here at my secret place... and why have you brought Christopher here', said Balish. Christopher felt reassured on hearing that his brother wasn't around him this all time. 'Secret place... are you doing some venture? But no lecturer did offer us a project, so why are you talking about a secret place', said Mora peculiarly.

'Oops', thought Balish when he turned the point very quickly and confidently, 'Oh sorry friend... I was talking about a Quidditch meeting at a secret place... and I and Werchiles were talking...then I thought to fetch some food and then... you inadvertently froze me'.

'Oh sorry that I doubted you... ok so you are talking about a secret place... hmmm, can I join you both right now... see I have only half an hour more, so please tell fast', said Mora.

Balish was stuck. How could he take Mora to his secret place where he was going to live then onwards? And lamentably, he had to put his charm on Mora and Christopher. They got frozen for a day and he took both of them and put in Mora's bed, as he wasn't returning to his old home especially to put Christopher in his bed.

Alfred was getting impatient now. He was just about to take-off on his broomstick to find Balish, when he returned with only water.

'Oh finally you've returned Balish. You know, I was about to go to find you, but you have come at the right time. By the way, where's the food', said Alfred.

'Be thankful to God that I have come with water', said Balish as he told the whole story what happened during that time with Balish.

Mr. Lane left a chuckle as he patted him, 'No problem Balish my boy. When we have your wand, then what is the need to worry? I know a modus operandi to bring food from your wand. You know, when I was a child, I once peeked into a wizards' class, where only wizards were taking their classes. And the most interesting fact was that the chapter that they were learning was the spell that I'm going to tell you so that we get food but I need your wand... So the spell was... ummm zeee..... yes 'Foodo'! A lot of food came in front of them. Alfred was so astonished that he put his hands over his mouth, 'Whoa man! What a trick sir'!

Mr. Lane glinted and asked Balish such a question, which though wasn't outrageous for Balish, but for mainly Mr. Lane himself.

'Er... Balish my boy, you told your single name, but what is your second name'? Thanks to God, Balish also asked the same question.

'Hahaha... I also forgot to ask your full name. On your door board there is some type of jotting, but it is very fainted... what's your full name'?

'Wait a minute guys... you both can say your full names together without wasting any time', said Alfred in the middle of their squabble.

'Ok...'

'Ok then...'

'Balish Lane

'Angus Lane

'Wha...What did you say you both... LANE, said Alfred, astonished as ever.

They were face-to-face. The father and son were in front of each other. They both couldn't understand what's happening here, but yes...they had understood this that they had a certain relationship, when Balish told the fake story about Angus that Mrs. Lane had told him.

'That means you are my... SON'!

'That means you are my... FATHER'!

They hugged each other, and when Mr. Lane asked about Balish's mother, and then Balish left a cry. 'The Inferno Lord had killed her ruthlessly... actually he wanted to kill ME... but mom sacrificed her life in order to save me... what an unlucky son am I'. He paused and then said again, 'Wait... if mother had told me that you were not alive, and all the 12 years I am not living with you, then where were we these years? Why did we part...? Dad... You have to tell me the whole story and right now'.

Angus sighed and hit his hands over his head a few times.

'Actually - the blameworthy is me. I hated children since they were so scrawny and you are not even our child...'

'WHAT! I AM NOT YOUR CHILD TOO'!

'Balish... if you hear the story quietly, then you will understand. One day, when I was going for my morning walk, then you were on our doorstep, and I refused to adopt you. As your mother had a lot of love towards you, she decided to adopt you, even if she had to part with me. And since she chose you, we broke relationship. And then onwards, she lived her life with you, and I lived my life alone, suffering the remorse I caused'.

Alfred guzzled quietly, while tears were undulating down Balish's cheeks.

'No... I can't live here... I am alive just to take revenge from Inferno Lord, and I'm not going to pass time with you... Mr. Guilty' and saying so he took out his wand and flew away.

Alfred also left a fake smile, as he departed leaving Mr. Lane alone.

Obviously he was anguishing the chastisement for his conduct, and he left Balish inconsolable than ever. He was wandering like a ghost in the sky, very above the sight of the normal man on his wand, when Alfred came and patted him on the back from behind, which petrified Balish for a jiffy.

'Don't you fret Balish... everything will be fine soon... but unfortunately you will have to return home, as you can't upset Mrs. Laurence. She must be waiting for you, as she knows you can't distress her', said Alfred to give valor to Balish.

'Ok - as you wish my friend... but you also return home as fast as you can. Mrs. Jones must be waiting for you, said Balish as they parted ways. Balish entered Mora's room, where Christopher was lying frozen on his bed. No one had probably noticed him. He quietly took Christopher in his laps and he made Mora normal by putting another de-freezing charm on him.

The next morning, when Christopher was rubbing his eyes, he was irate to find Balish lying on his bed.

'YOU HERE'!

'Oh yea bro, after all it's my home', said Balish.

'I'm sure that I'm dreaming, for the reason that the Balish whom I saw with a clear view had gone from this home and forever'... said Christopher when Mrs. Laurence suddenly entered the room and saw Balish sitting there. 'Balish! You are here! I ...cannot believe it'... Said Mrs. Laurence.

'Aunt, I've not come to stay here... instead I have come to warn Christopher not to rib me whenever I'm around you, when I come to see you- so don't have the misinterpretation that this orphan will stay here... Oh by the word of orphan, I have an idea... I can stay in an orphanage. Far away from this place where no taunts will be reverberating in my ears, so bye', said Balish.

He took out his wand and flew from there. On the other side, Mrs. Laurence slapped Christopher very tightly, who was still blatant.

'Who cares about that boy... after all he said correct, he's an'...

Mrs. Laurence slapped Christopher once again and shut his mouth by her hands.

'NEVER SAY THAT DIRTY THING'...

'I WILL... HE IS AN ORPHAN, AND NO ONE CAN REFUSE THIS TRUTH', said Christopher. Then only Alfred entered through the windowpane and said. 'Oh really Christopher - I can prove you wrong, and what happened to your bet which you said... you would click a picture of the Inferno Lord and bring it to us'.

'Mom, I'm getting late for school, I'm off. You both, if want to continue to argue, then argue'. Mrs. Laurence patted Alfred on the back. 'He's immature. Leave him alone and after some time he will be fine as before'. Alfred sighed and left for school.

To everyone's surprise, Christopher was standing with a loudspeaker in his hand on the assembly stage. Mr. Hulhuge, when entered in the hall, was staggered too. 'Mr. Laurence, I think you have forgotten the rule that without mine or the headmistress's permission, you cannot step on this stage'.

'Sir, I know that, but I want to tell you a thing'...

'No fads or things. You have broken the rules, by hook or by crook, and you will get the punishment. You should meet me before leaving for home, said Mr. Hulhuge.

Balish quickly understood that Christopher wanted to tell his truth, that he was an orphan. Mr. Hulhuge forgave Christopher this time when he fell on his feet for confession.

When he was returning, he stopped Christopher.

'Oh brother, what do you want, why are you again and again going against me? Am I your enemy? If yes, then tell me truthfully. I'll leave right now, but don't share my personal status to everyone, please'.

Christopher was a bit emotional, and after Balish solicited for the answer, he said. 'Hmmm, so at least you are successful to persuade me to tell the answer. You are not my enemy, not at all. But as you see, you are a wizard, which I am not. You are staying in my home, and my mom is paying more attention to you. So I want you to give, or help me in getting an idea that how can mom give equal attention to both of us, and that should finish in less than a month'.

Balish was a semi-wizard, and he knew better. He thought for a minute and then patted him on the shoulder.

'Ok then. This will also help you to execute the bet... remember?

Christopher jumped very high and hugged Balish. At last, the adversary of Christopher turned again in brotherhood.

'But for that, you'll have to be brave and courageous. No trepidation should enter your body. Because we're going to examine the under-construction building', said Balish with fire of revenge burning in his eyes.

* * *

– CHAPTER –

10

Enemy-Enemy, Face to Face

Y...you mean that we're going to face the In... Inferno lo...lord'? Said Christopher with sweat trickling all over his head.

Balish nodded and in a fraction of a second, he was on his way towards the forest.

'N...Nooooo Balish! Not today! We...we have a month. Some other day, please', said Christopher, trying not to show his apprehension but it was quickly understood by Balish.

'Ho-Hum, okay then. We'll wait for a week, but then we will go. And don't feel alone. Even I have to kill that cruel devil. I want revenge, which I will try to achieve. I will not let innocent children become the hunt anymore. After 7 days, either he will die, or I', said Balish with the fire of revenge still burning with full action.

Suddenly after reaching home, Balish's scratch started itching. It was unbearable, but Balish knew the reason of that itching.

'Dears, come quickly, your lunch is ready, said Mrs. Laurence to the duo, who were in deep thoughts of the Inferno Lord.

After having lunch (only bread with peanut margarine), Balish took his mini-laptop and went in his room. On one side, Balish was finding the cure of the itch which was increasing, and on the other side, Christopher was finding a way to defeat the Inferno Lord, which wasn't mentioned anywhere in the wizsites.

There he was, in the building in front of Inferno Lord. He was holding a wand, though he wasn't capable of attacking him.

'Hey boy, get ready for your death... Conflagirosta'.........

'NOOOOOOO'!

'What happened to you Christopher'?! Said Balish, rubbing his eyes.

'Leave me, leave me... It was Balish's idea... not my...'

'Christopher, I'm Balish'. Christopher left a huge sigh, but relaxed after a few seconds. 'Balish... I am not going with you in that building. I don't want to die so fast. You do whatever you want to do'. Balish got angry and put Christopher's hand on his head.

'For the sake of friendship and brotherhood, you will go with me', and saying so, he went to sleep. 'But how can you do this Balish'? Until then, Balish had slept.

The next day, Balish asked Christopher, 'Ok. What if I include Alfred in our plan? Then you're not alone. Hmmm'? Christopher agreed, and that day only, Balish went to Alfred's house and heaved him lovingly in the backyard. Balish whispered the plan to Alfred, who hi-fived Balish at once, which surprised Christopher. For the next 6 days, they hardly studied and on the 7th day, they all went in the forest, throwing their bags on the doorsteps of their homes and holding wands in their hands.

'Are...Are you sure that we will be safe'? Said Christopher, who alone was scared among the trio.

'Oh Christopher, I forgot to bring my water bottle, can you please bring it for me'? Said Balish, who had planned a surprise for Christopher and his fear.

'Oh thanks. I will take my time and bring the bottle... any problem'? Said Christopher.

'Not at all', said Balish.

Christopher whistled while going home and at home, just beside the water bottle, there was a box on which it was written, 'OPEN'. Just as he opened it, a very common thing was inside it. A spring mask jumped in front of Christopher's face, which surprised him. There was a letter on which someone had written 2 sentences in rough handwriting.

Nothing will happen. We are there with you and nothing will happen to you.

The name of the writer wasn't mentioned, but Christopher knew it was none other than Balish who had written this letter.

He ran towards them and waved to Balish from a particular point.

'There he comes. See now, his face is brighter and he is looking confident', said Balish with a wink to Alfred, but as he turned behind, he wasn't there. Christopher was in front of Balish, and in a fraction of a second, he flew in the air as if some magnetic power is pulling him towards itself.

'Christopherrr'! screamed Balish who held his legs, but suddenly he felt a great shock in his hands and the grip was lost. He cried for help and ran behind Christopher, who had already disappeared in the dense trees with his faint yells of help.

Balish got tired after a few minutes, when he realized that why didn't he fly on his wand? How could he be so stupid? Now what answer would he give to Mrs. Laurence? He then flew on his wand above the branches of the trees thinking that Christopher must have stuck in some branch, but it was too late. He was away. Balish zapped and after a distance, he noticed that the under-construction building was not there. The cement was still on the gentle grass but the building was not there.

'CHRISTOPHERrrrr'! CHRISTOPHERrrrr... CHRISTOPHERrrr

Balish's voice echoed and he knew that now he is in the middle of the forest.

The wind started gusting and birds like crows flew above the trees. This was an indication that a great storm is going to come. Suddenly, a sound came. Balish thought it was Christopher's, but the voice was stronger and rougher. Balish left a gulp. He strongly recognized that voice. It was none other's than the Inferno Lord's.

'My boy, let's talk carefully in our hidey-hole', said the Inferno Lord, and when Balish tried to look where the sound was coming from, he also flew in the air. Balish was so tensed that he couldn't shoot any spell or put a freeze charm anywhere. His hands were tightly held and he fell with a 'DOOM' on the floor. There Alfred and Christopher were stuck on the ceiling and Balish came to know that this was the same under-construction building, where Jack and his family was killed by the Inferno Lord.

Faint voices of shrieks were heard by the trio. Balish told them not to panic, but now even Alfred was looking scared.

'So... Balish, you are the boy who escaped from my master last time, but this time I will finish you off and sacrifice your head in front of my lord', said a woman in front of Balish.

When he got up, he was shocked to see that the women who said the verdict was looking like his own mother, Mrs. Rita Lane. Balish said," Mom...

'Mom'! 'Are you crazy? I am not your mom. Yes, you must be surprised that this face is your mom's, but actually the ashes of your mom flung in the air and fell straight on me at the time of her death. And since then I am your mother's soul', said she. 'Don't forget that I have come here to take revenge from your stupid master, not you. Where has that scared rat hid', said Balish with confidence.

His scratch started burning this time, and the colour also changed from jet black to pure orange. Balish fell on the ground, and with a slight shriek, lay motionless. From the ceiling, Christopher and Alfred started crying and shouting, though tape was on their mouths. That woman dragged Balish out of that room and took him in another room. 'Master... here's your hunt who escaped from you last time'...

But from the behind, a purple jet of light hit her on the chest and she fell dead. Mora had come to the rescue and he took Balish upto the main door where Christopher and Alfred were happy, but then the door closed and locked on its own. Balish woke up and saw Mora in front of him.

'Mora... you here? But how did you come to know that we are here'?

'When Christopher was bringing your water bottle, I was on the windowpane and I spotted him. After that I followed him and so on and so on... but now it is time for us to flee from this place anyhow. You help in disentangling Christopher and Alfred, and I find a place to go out of this place.

Just then, Mora also flew in the air and got stuck on the ceiling in no time.

'Moraaaa'!

'You don't worry about me. You find a place to go out, I am here to handle the matter', said Mora when a strong strip of tape pressed his mouth tight.

'No ways, I am not going to go from here... I have come to take revenge and I will take revenge, even if I lose my life', said Balish.

'Oh really! Then ok, let's play a fair game. I won't hurt your scratch', said the Inferno Lord from behind, but just as Balish turned behind, he was disappeared.

This time he shouted, 'THIS IS NOT A DRAMA THAT I WILL NOT KILL YOU AND SPARE YOU, THAT ALSO AFTER SUCH A LONG TIME... Conflagirostaaaaaa'!

A jet of red fire just missed the fast Balish.

He again shouted, '**Conflagirosta** ...

But just then Balish had spotted his back and he shouted, 'LEISTACIO'!!!!

What had happened? The Inferno Lord fell down on the ground, causing a bit of tremble in the earth.

'Christopher, Mora, Alfred'... said Balish and he released them with quick succession.

They were released but Balish's scratch started burning again. He fell again, but he wasn't motionless. He shouted a lot when Mora put some cool water on his scratch, which was now hurting lesser. But unlike the spell, Inferno Lord had got up. He was on his feet and the duo was face-to-face finally.

Christopher, just after looking his white-ghostlike face, hid behind an empty box with fear. 'What happened boy? Stunned? Well ok. You and your two

rats, Alfred and Mora can join you in your team. But me and my huge army will fight with me', said Inferno Lord.

Then only black creatures appeared from the corners of the room, in a line. Mora, Alfred and Balish

were holding their wands and fighting the uncountable creatures, which were called ZERTIAS. They were dying with one stroke of the wands, but as they were uncountable, they were coming nearer and nearer and had filled the room, just leaving a small circle where the trio was standing. At the top, the Inferno Lord was laughing very loudly, which made Christopher more scared.

Now Balish had an idea. He quickly whispered in Christopher and Alfred's ears, and they shouted in quick successions.

'LEISTACIO! LEISTACIO! LEISTACIO'!

The zertias had frozen and fallen on the ground. But suddenly another huge bunch of zertias came from the corners and started approaching the trio.

Balish thought and thought when he got another idea. He whispered again and Mora and Alfred flew on their wands. They went on the corners and put strong strips of double-sided icy tape on the walls, which stopped the flow of the zertias.

Even the Inferno Lord was stunned. The remaining zertias had been finished by Balish very easily.

Now was the time for the Inferno Lord to fight. He clapped in anger for the trio.

'Well done rats! You are successful to escape from my army, but right now the leader is still here... 'And we will escape through this big hole too', said Balish with great anger.

'Great Balish, but can you imagine what a death I will give you? Okay, before sending you up, I will teach you some etiquette. So first of all, you have to touch my feet and show your respect towards elders', said Inferno Lord.

'Never, you stupid fellow, and don't try to teach us etiquettes. Right now we will teach you the correct manners by finishing you off.

'I've been kind to you since a long time, and now it is time to finish my hunt. And yes, now I have 3 more hunts. That's called 'buy one get 3 free'. Hahaha... hahahaha', said the Inferno Lord.

He shouted 'Leistacio'! The jet of ice zoomed towards the trio, when they clicked their wands together and shouted, 'LEISTACIO'! The ice transformed into dust, which made the Inferno Lord furious. He shouted once more, and probably the last time, 'Conflagirosta'!

This time they threw their wands in the fire together, which caused the fire to become a huge blast.

The wand from the Inferno Lord's hand slipped and fell in the jet of the red fire. 'What have you done you silly boys? Don't you know the punishment I'll give you for this mistake'? Said the Inferno Lord.

'But how will you beat us without your wand... Mora, Alfred... you know what to do now', said Balish, his fire of revenge now making Balish raged. They all fisted their hands and came nearer to the Inferno Lord, who, for the first time looked tensed.

'You didn't think the punishment I would give you for you finished my mother ruthlessly'? Said Balish, now tears of fury in his eyes.

'But I didn't want to kill her... I wanted to kill you, but don't think I'm unarmed', said the Inferno Lord as he took a spade out of his dusty cloak.

Balish quickly jumped on his wand and flew over the Inferno Lord's head, and pulled him by the head into the air.

'Leave me'...

Mora and Alfred were triumphant in snatching the spade from his hand, and they called Christopher from behind the box.

Christopher sneaked and then his fear disappeared. He quickly took his mini-top in his hand and was about to take a photo of the struggling dark wizard, when Balish refused.

'Not now Christopher... when he is on the ground and begging for life, then make a video'. Christopher winked as Balish reached the ceiling and Mora broke the ceiling by a lightning charm.

Balish took him towards the city.

'No Balish... my reputation is at stake... please Balish... leave me... I ask for mercy... please', beseeched the sweating Inferno Lord. 'Ok then, if your reputation is at stake, then I can finish you off by throwing you down from here'...

Just then Mora zapped by and pulled the Inferno Lord by the legs and went back to the building, safely dropping him on the floor.

'YOU'RE DOOMED CHILD... I HAVE A SPARE WAND WITH ME... THIS WAS MY PLAN... AND I AM VICTORIUS NOW... Conflagirosta'...

Mora quickly reacted and put a charm of supersonic power which interrupted the jet of fire in midair. He snatched the wand from his hand, when Balish and Alfred came to the spot.

'Beat him until he's dead. Yes Christopher; take a video of this merciless criminal'. Christopher made a video, in which the Inferno Lord was bleeding and breathing profoundly.

'Ok then, let's start... 3... 2... 1...'

Inferno Lord shouted 'NO' but now it was too late. The trio had already started beating him very callously. Blood was trickling from the face of the Inferno Lord, whose eyes were about to be closed forever.

After 2 minutes, he was motionless. The trio stopped beating. Christopher's hands were on his mouth.

'I think he's over. Let's show our trophy of victory to the people', said Balish.

They took him on their wands (Balish held his head, Alfred his legs and Mora his shoulders). The people saw them. In less than a minute, a huge crowd appeared around the body of the Inferno Lord. Reporters started clashing to take photos of their heroes and the Inferno Lord. But, whether it was a an illusion or fact, some fingers of the Inferno lord were moving...

At home, Mrs. Laurence was looking the news when Balish's face appeared. Then the Inferno Lord was shown. Mrs. Laurence called Mr. Laurence and they appeared at the place where almost half of the city had already gathered.

'Oh Balish, are you fine? And what happened to the Inferno Lord? Said she. 'I have taken revenge. I have taken revenge. I have taken revenge... now my mother's soul will rest in peace', said Balish, still angry.

'Balish, control yourself. You've done a very heroic and brave deed. No one knows how many children have been the hunts of this wizard, but now everyone is safe. Let's go home, Iogy's waiting for you, said Mr. Laurence, who appeared out of the blue.

All was well. The consternation in everyone's mind was disappeared. Now Balish and his team were known as the 'champions of the city', and all the city people, especially all the children, were free to roam in the forest and enjoy their life and nature without any fear.

* * *